WINGED

PASSION

Heaven's Heart

WINGED PASSION

Book Three

AMANDA PILLAR

Published by Maatkare Books
www.amandapillar.com

Editor: Pete Kemsphall

ISBN: 978-0-6480295-8-8

Cover Design: Yocla Book Cover Designs © 2018
Internal Layout: Amanda Pillar © 2019
Editor: Pete Kempshall

First Published February 2019

To Hayley — sister of the heart.

CHAPTER 1

Seven Months Earlier...

"I love your strength, your loyalty, and your beauty. I want to spend the rest of my life with you." Paschar's cerulean-blue eyes gleamed with passion, his voice low and intense. His musician's hand clasped Seraphina's, his grip tight, fervent. His wings arched behind him, their pure white feathers soft as the finest silk.

Emotion clogged Seraphina's throat. She'd been waiting for this day for years. Decades, even. Ever since she had asked Paschar to marry her, and he had kindly and reluctantly refused, she had bided her time, waiting for him to be ready. She had her role in the military, he explained, and he was busy creating music for their race.

What has changed?

She met Paschar's bright gaze, noting the brilliance of his golden hair, the perfectly chiseled jaw, the confident manner in which he held himself.

Her voice soft, gentle, she said, "I love you, too."

She had been in love with him for what felt like

forever. They had been lovers for five decades, and yet this was the first truly ardent declaration he had ever made her.

God had spoken true when he'd said patience was a virtue.

Over the arch of Paschar's wings, the sparse walls of her room were an inadequate frame for such a moment; her bed, nightstand and bookshelf spoke of austerity, rather than rich emotion. Such a grand moment needed an equally grand setting.

This will have to do.

It was all she had, after all. Warriors were noble of spirit, and poor of material possessions. One could not be weighed down by pesky things such as covetousness or jealously if one never had much to begin with.

Paschar smiled, satisfaction underlying the expression. "I knew you would agree to marry me."

You didn't actually ask.

She opened her mouth to point that out, but he spoke first; "Before we marry, I must admit that my family has a secret shame." He glanced at the ground, his mouth set in a grim line.

Seraphina paused, then withdrew her hand slowly. Why had he not spoken of this before? More than half a century together, and *this* was the first time he talked of family problems? She had told him all of her secrets—not that there were many.

When he didn't elaborate, she patted him on the leg. "I am listening."

He jerked his head up, stare narrowing. "You already judge me."

"No, I do not judge; that is for God. I just wonder why

you have waited so long to tell me. You know I will never hold your family's actions against you."

"I had to be sure of your feelings—of your commitment to *me*—first."

Like she had failed to make that plain before.

"I love you, you can hear the truth in my words."

Being angels, they had an in-built lie-detector. He would know if she falsely professed love, if she didn't feel it. And how could she not, when confronted with the force of nature that was Paschar?

He was given to great emotions; everything was wonderful, or everything was dreadful. It could be exhausting at times, but it was part of why she loved him: he was intensity and desire and fierceness. Sometimes it made him highly strung, but she had chosen to love him, flaws as well as perfections.

He took a deep breath and exhaled slowly. "I had a brother, Cassiel."

Surprise shot through her. Did he think she wouldn't have heard of Cassiel? Did he believe her that naïve?

Paschar had always been spoken of as if he were an only child, but it was not uncommon for parents to choose to renounce fallen children—to act as if that child had never been born. And she'd been aware that Paschar's mother had had a fallen child from a previous union.

"He was a liar and a cheat. He deliberately flaunted Heaven's rules and was banished for the act. My parents have never gotten over the shame—but this happened a long time ago. I was barely fifty years old.

"His wings were excised, and he was expelled from Heaven, never to return." Something mean and hard twisted Paschar's expression for a moment, before his face smoothed back to its normal handsomeness.

"I have heard of Cassiel," she said. "He aided a demon, did he not?"

Cassiel's fall had happened before her birth. It had been rarely talked about, but every now and then, the story of the angel who would rather help a demon than kill it was used to warn young angels about the folly of compassion for any Hell-spawn.

Still, was it a crime worthy of being cast out?

No, do not think such things. The archangels speak the word of God. They would only do what is just, what is fair.

Paschar seemed to be waiting for her to say something.

"I am so sorry your family had to go through that. You must have missed your brother at the time."

"Missed a traitor?" Paschar's words were short, clipped. "No. But you are kind to think of such a thing. Always thinking the best of people. It is a trait I admire."

Truth. But not the whole truth.

Was he being sarcastic?

"But why wait to tell me such a thing until now?" she asked.

"Because I could not bear for you to think less of me." He took hold of her hand again. "Do you?"

"Of course not." It was not his behavior that had resulted in Heaven's laws being broken, but his brother's, although, she did wish he had trusted her before now. It was something they could have worked through, together.

He gave her a soft kiss on the cheek, the press of his lips fleeting. "Our marriage will not impact your placement in the Darts?"

"No. Dina has made it clear that my position is secure."

Seraphina had once been a scout for the archangel Gabriel, but had recently been made a member of an elite squadron run by a fierce warrior-angel called Dina. Together, the six Darts protected Heaven's Heart, one of angelkind's most treasured possessions.

"Excellent. I am so glad they awarded you such an esteemed role. It has been the talk of the town for years." Satisfaction glimmered in Paschar's eyes. "With your placement, and my talent, nothing will stop us rising together as stars. Nothing."

Seraphina flinched as the archangel Michael laid a heavy hand on Azrael's shoulder. The pair of them kneeled beside two other Darts on the charred and ash-smeared ground before the Inner Sanctum, the former home of Heaven's Heart. The door to the sacred chamber had been blasted open and the scent of blood and ozone was thick in the air.

The Celestial City had been breached by demons and now Heaven's Heart was missing, as were its on-duty guards, Dina and Zadkiel.

Michael spoke quietly, but fury saturated his every word. "You will *all* be punished for this."

On their knees before him, Raziel, Yael, Azrael and Seraphina bowed their heads.

"Do you know who breached the walls?" Raziel asked.

"At this stage, it does not matter who attacked us," Michael replied.

Surprise seared through her. *How* could it not be important? They needed to rescue Dina and Zadkiel—to restore the Heart. Knowing the identity of their attackers was but the first step in what would no doubt be a long journey.

"Heaven's Heart has been stolen. Do you understand what you've all done?"

Nothing, she thought. *We've done nothing.*

Only two angels were required to protect the Heart at any given time—this had been decreed by the archangels themselves. The Darts took turns, rotating so that the Inner Sanctum was never unguarded. Seraphina had not been in the hall; it would have been impossible for her to provide assistance.

"Sire," Raziel murmured, "if you will let us search, we will find the Heart and bring it back."

Michael's long brown hair swung over his shoulder, the braid brushing over his robes as he moved. His eyes were pure white, with no iris or pupil, and massive wings soared over his shoulders, their white expanse thickly threaded with gold—the marker that he was an archangel. "Oh, you will search for the Heart," he said. "But first, you must pay the price for your failure." A huge sword appeared in his right hand, the blade gleaming.

Seraphina's mind went blank as panic gripped her. Automatically, she went to stand, but magic kept her on her knees, rooted to the floor.

Another archangel strode in front of them; Uriel in his golden robe, his ebony skin glinting with blue highlights.

A pulse of power told her that more archangels had arrived. Fear pounded in her blood.

"Word of this will have reached all of Heaven before sunset. Examples must be made."

"Examples?" Seraphina hadn't meant to speak, but the word escaped before she could stop it.

Michael stepped closer, his white gaze pitiless. "You will all be exiled from Heaven."

Exiled.

She would have to leave Paschar, her family, her friends...

"You will only be allowed to return if you find all three pieces of the Heart and give them to us," Michael continued.

"All *three* pieces?" Yael asked.

A short silence. "We guarded but one part of the Heart," Michael said. "It is time all three were rejoined and stored here for safety."

Confusion warred with fear and hope. They could earn their way back into Heaven. She could one day fly over the Celestial City, be with her family once more.

This was only temporary.

They *had* to find all three pieces.

"Can you give us any information on what we might seek?" Raziel asked.

Michael shook his head. "This is a punishment. We will not help you with it."

"Then we shall leave at once, so we may find the stolen piece and its brethren." Raziel's tone was filled with purpose.

"There is something else that must be done first," Uriel said.

She watched as, without warning, Azrael was shoved face-down onto the blood-stained marble floor. Seraphina gasped as a strong hand grabbed one of his wings, holding it out straight, exposing the part where the tendons met the back muscles.

No. They would not do this...

Then someone was pushing her forward, cracking her cheek against the ground. Rough hands grabbed her wings, and then agony burst through her, the pain so razor-sharp her vision turned gray and her heart stopped beating for a handful of seconds. *Breathe, breathe,* she told herself, but the air would not come, the torture relentless.

Then it was over.

The magic that had held her in place vanished, but she remained on the ground, panting, her skin on fire and her back screaming. Wings shot with silver threads were kicked into her line of vision, and she reached out, her shaking fingers brushing against the bloody stumps that had once joined living flesh.

She had been an angel.

Now she was nothing.

CHAPTER 2

Seraphina's wings were gone. No evidence remained of her race except for the healing gashes on either side of her spine.

White hot pain still scored her back, even though the mutilation had happened hours ago. A single, silver-threaded feather lay in her hands, the only remnant she had of her once beautiful plumage.

The archangel Gabriel had not commented on her the feather, a treasure she was forbidden to possess, after he'd teleported the Darts to the Human Realm. Instead, he'd gently touched her shoulder, sadness in his violet eyes. Then he'd gone, abandoning them to their fate.

Carefully, she lay the feather on the duvet next to her, before pulling her legs up to her chest, wincing as the movement stretched the healing wounds on her back.

What was a little more discomfort?

The room around her slowly swam into focus. Decorated with navy blue and cream tones, it was as lush and elegant as her former rooms had been spartan and ascetic. A four-poster bed dominated the space, with a mahogany desk decorated in gold leaf set diagonally across from her. A small sofa was propped against the wall to her left and a walk-in-robe and private bathroom were directly opposite.

This room would have pleased Paschar. It was just to his taste; delicately luxurious. She'd no idea that Raziel owned such an immense property, and in the Human Realm, no less. He had explained about their accommodations after they had been exiled from Heaven, but she could barely remember what he'd said.

It's your new home, she thought.

Laying her head on her arms, tears escaped, wetting her cheeks. Just hours earlier, she had thought this was one of the best days of her life. Now her dreams lay shattered around her, like the remnants of the Inner Sanctum's door.

At least I have Paschar. He will wait for me. He loves me.

"How could you?!"

She jerked upright, wiping distractedly at her cheeks. "Paschar?"

Gratitude and pleasure shot through her at the sight of her lover, his beautiful wings flaring behind him, a breathtaking sweep of white against the dark blue room.

"How could you do this to me?" he demanded, stepping forward.

Finally, his words registered, stabbing into her like a knife wound to her kidney. "What do you mean?" She edged her legs off the bed, put her feet on the floor.

"Look at you! You're a disgrace. You've made me a laughing stock. My parents are horrified."

A new kind of pain beat through her. He meant every word.

"You said you loved me, that we'd be together forever." She felt brittle, like she might break into a million shards at any second.

"I can't be with you. You're *exiled*." He paced.

"This is not permanent," she said. "We have been given a task, so that we can return to Heaven. If you wait—"

"Wait? For what? For you to fail like you did today?"

Seraphina clutched at her chest, the words tearing and scarring her heart.

"You're worthless to me now," he muttered.

Worthless.

Had he only wanted to be with her because he'd valued her position in their society?

Her breath seized in her lungs. She forced herself to inhale. "Then why bother coming here?"

"I had to make sure that you wouldn't embarrass me further by coming to meet me."

Embarrass him? She was the one who had lost her wings, her family, her life. "I—"

"And just after I told you about my brother. Didn't you think about me at all?"

"No, no I didn't. I was too busy having my wings cut off." The venom in her voice made him pause. But not for long.

"You should have considered my feelings."

"Really?" she spat. "When exactly should I have thought about your precious reputation? When I was learning that demons had raided Heaven? When I watched my comrades get their wings cut off? Or when I was being exiled from Heaven?"

Paschar's blue eyes darkened. "You should have

begged for mercy! You should have denied any involvement!"

"We *weren't* involved. And the archangels were not given to mercy. You think they would have spared me if I'd mentioned *your* name?"

He didn't seem to hear her derision. "They may have."

What a fool. Paschar was a gifted musician, she would give him that, but he was not so popular that the archangels asked him to perform for them on a regular basis.

"But would you have still wanted me, if they had decided to spare me alone?" she muttered.

"Of course."

He was lying. She could taste it, smell it, even. Rage such as she'd never known filled her; this betrayal cut deeper than the blade that had stolen her wings.

He'd told her he loved her. That he wanted forever with her.

But his love was not unconditional, and therefore it was not real.

"Get. Out."

His eyebrows drew together sharply. "Excuse me?"

"Get out of my room."

"I was leaving anyway. I just came to ask you to tell no one of my proposal."

As if she would. To think, she had wasted fifty years on him. Still... "Why?"

"There is no need for two lives to be destroyed this day."

Two lives? Try *six.*

"I see."

"I'm glad you do. For once, please do the right thing

by me."

And then he was gone.

For once? She thought back over the past fifty years, at all the times she had forgiven his tardiness, his moodiness, his selfishness. She had *constantly* done right by him, making excuses, being overly courteous to compensate.

It was only now that she could see it hadn't been reciprocated.

He thinks I am worthless.

No, she thought furiously, straightening her spine despite the physical ache. *I'm worth more than you can ever imagine.*

CHAPTER 3

Present day

Trick had had a bad week. Hell, he was going to call it and say he'd had a bad month.

And Trick had long ago decided that bad days were for everyone else.

But fate had a way of sucker-punching you when you least expected it. First, his former slave and friend, Dru, had bought her freedom. Then she'd threatened to kill him because he'd sold her twin sister, Peony, to the Mortus. Like it was anything other than a business decision. Said twin had then gone and murdered the Mortus king and taken his crown for herself, making her queen of the Mortus and someone who you shouldn't fuck with, ever. And all while these shenanigans were going on, the angel he'd purchased out of pity from a bunch of Infernus demons had escaped, only to turn up in Hell...by Peony's side.

Now the winged asshole was refusing to return to the Halcyon Guild.

Trick rubbed his forehead. *I think I am getting a headache.*

His species didn't even *get* headaches.

The door to his office slammed open, and Dru stood there, her white hair tied back in a bun, and her gray eyes aflame. She was dressed in blue jeans and a black tank top, a sight so familiar that it sent a pang through Trick's deadened heart. For a moment, hope flared that she had decided to return—as a free member of the guild, rather than a slave. But from her thunderous frown, he quickly realized that this was unlikely.

"Trick."

"That is my name." He drummed his fingers over the surface of his desk, one of the two pieces of furniture in the room. This place was for him, not for others. Anyone who set foot in his domain *should* feel uncomfortable, and he'd furnished the room to ensure they did. Plus, he didn't use his office for meetings frequently—he liked the guild thinking that he conducted most of his business within their purview. It made them more comfortable around him, more willing to do his bidding.

Well, that *had* been the case until he'd sold Peony to the Mortus. He was still putting out the fires that had erupted after that decision.

Like I'd had a choice. When the spawn of Satan come knocking, you answer the door promptly. Trick hadn't wanted to start a diplomatic incident. Sure, he didn't answer to Satan, but the Hell-lord could make waves for Hades, and Hades was someone Trick *did* have to worry about. After all, the Halcyon Guild's headquarters were in the former god's realm, Tartarus.

"Are you going to invite me in?" Dru asked, voice dry.

"I didn't think you were going to wait for an invitation." She never had before.

She strode into his office like she owned it, leaning her hip against his desk; there was no chair on her side. "Still an asshole, I see."

"It's been, what, four weeks since you left? Why'd you expect anything different?" He leaned back in his seat, the banter familiar and strangely comforting.

"Miracles can happen."

"Yeah, like your sister killing the Mortus king. Who knew she had it in her?"

Dru's gray eyes bled to entirely black and a pulse of pure evil tingled over his skin. But when she spoke, her voice was calm. "About that...we need to talk."

"I can't buy her back, and I wouldn't, even if I could. Peony will be good for the Mortus."

She really would. Dru's twin had an inner moral compass that most demons lacked. She'd help them sort their shit out, and the Mortus would no doubt become the most efficient—and feared—race of demons in all three circles of Hell.

Actually, they were already the most feared.

He'd chosen to sell Peony rather than her sister simply because he'd thought her chances of surviving in the Mortus den were higher than Dru's. His former assassin had a tendency of killing first, asking questions later. Which, you know, was too late, since she didn't have necromancy in her skillset.

"It's not about Peony exactly," Dru hedged.

He sighed. "You're here about the damned angel."

Z.

That fucker had just disappeared from the cells one

day—the same day Dru had left the guild for good, so he could do the math—and had ignored Trick's magical summons for three weeks. Most demons would have come crawling back from the pain by now.

But not this angel.

Prick.

"Yes," Dru said. "Actually no. Not me, exactly."

He frowned. "What do you mean?"

"I kind of brought someone with me; she's waiting outside. I'll let her explain." She strode to the door, opened it, and left.

A second later, a statuesque woman with midnight-black skin stood in the open doorway. Her hair hung to her waist in a multitude of braids, and she was dressed in a power suit, complete with a briefcase. She looked like a lawyer. She was far worse.

She was a fallen angel, and a member of the rival Falling Star mercenary guild.

He groaned.

"Trick." Her voice dripped poison that rivaled bloomshade, one of the deadliest Hell-plants in all the realms.

"Seraphina."

This woman was the face of the Falling Star—beautiful beyond belief, she charmed her way through clients, winning contract after contract. He'd gone to a party hosted by her guild a month ago, and had been suitably impressed by the group's grandeur, and by her even more so.

But he knew what danger it was to mess with a woman who viewed men as nothing more than conquests. Perhaps that was why he'd had a thing for Dru for all these years. She didn't chew up lovers and spit them out afterward—she couldn't, since she every time she took someone to bed, they risked their life.

Still, he wasn't blind, and he could admire Seraphina's beauty despite her cold demeanor.

"To what do I owe the pleasure of your visit?" He leaned back in his chair, clasping his hands over his stomach.

She closed the door and strode to stand in front of his desk. "You will transfer the blood contract you have on Z to me."

He blinked.

Re-ran her statement in his mind, then blinked again.

"Sorry, I will do *what*?"

"I don't like repeating myself."

"Don't be ridiculous."

She placed the briefcase on his desk with a thunk, opened the clips with brisk efficiency, then held up several pieces of paper. "I have a copy of his contract here."

How'd she get that?

"So?"

"It says down here," she flicked to the second-last page, "that Z's debt can be transferred to another person. A life for a life."

He leaned forward, intrigued by the argument. "And like for like."

"Exactly. I am an angel, he is an angel. I would swap my life for his."

"But you don't have wings."

"I am still an angel."

"You are fallen, he is not."

Her chin jerked up. "If he went back to Heaven, he would have his wings removed and be cast out just the same."

"Again, he has wings."

"With toxic feathers. You couldn't sell them. Anyway, angel feathers lose potency if they grow in Hell."

His wings had turned poisonous?

Now *that* was something he hadn't known. But Z's presence in the Mortus den now made sense. He was likely to be Peony's mate.

Goddamn it.

Angels didn't have mates, but they could be someone else's, and that meant taking him back from the Mortus would cause an inter-Hell issue—the exact thing Trick had been trying to avoid when selling Peony to the damned demons in the first place.

He was between a rock and a hard place, and from the gleam in Seraphina's eyes, she knew it.

"So, while I may be wingless, I am still an angel. You won't get Z back willingly, and do you really want to take on the might of the Mortus to just prove a point? I am offering you a solution to your problem."

He narrowed his eyes. "Why?"

"Why what?"

"Why *are* you offering this solution? What do you get out of it?"

"I am doing this for Z. We were comrades in Heaven."

She was being honest, but not completely so. Considering how he liked to hold his cards close to his chest, he couldn't blame her. But privacy was not a thing he promoted—secrets put the guild, its slaves and its free members at risk.

"What about the Falling Star? You can't work for them and be a blood slave here at the same time."

The new mercenary guild had sprung up out of nowhere seven months previously, and had done very well, considering they lived in the Human Realm, and most of the work available was in Hell.

"I will resign my role."

Trick ran a hand over his hair, thinking hard. The only problem, he figured, was that he couldn't really see a way to refuse her offer.

"Fine."

Triumph flared in her dark-brown eyes.

"But let's seal the deal properly." Something wicked took hold of him. "With blood...and a kiss."

CHAPTER 4

A kiss?

Seraphina would not betray her dismay at Trick's demand. Sure, he was a handsome devil, with burnished gold hair and chocolate-brown eyes, but she didn't want to make out with the demon who would soon own her soul.

Call her crazy for wanting to keep the relationship strictly business.

"Too chicken?" he said, standing. "Worried you'll like it?"

She flicked her hair over her shoulder, defiance in every line of her posture. "I didn't say no, did I?"

Seraphina was tall, but Trick stood a few inches taller. Despite his smart business attire, the demon was packed with muscle and probably weighed a good fifty to sixty pounds more than she did. While she was a trained warrior, she wasn't sure she could take him in a fight; she was fast, but size did count for something in battle.

Funny how this is what you think of when a man tries to kiss you, rather than how soft his mouth would feel.

That's what she'd used to wonder about Paschar, before they had become lovers: how his lips would taste, how his body would feel pressed against hers...But look how that had worked out for her. Betrayed, left alone when she needed him most, and slandered in Heaven.

Oh, she wasn't meant to know about the latter, but she had heard the rumors, even working in the Human Realm as she did.

Trick came around the desk, a knife appearing in his hand as he stopped next to her. "Shall we sign first?"

"Of course."

If she had to kiss him, she wasn't about to do it without a contract in place. Although, why'd he'd want to kiss her, she didn't know. Maybe because she was exotic? A fallen angel for the newest notch in his no-doubt pock-holed belt?

He waved his free hand with a flourish, and a contract appeared, the paper yellowed as if with age. But the contract was new, only a few weeks' old, so she knew it couldn't be. *He's showy.* Trick placed it on the table, grabbed a pen, and crossed out Z's thumbprint.

He held out his palm. "Give me your hand."

She knew what he wanted, but she didn't like the idea of his blade cutting her skin without her being the one to wield it. She didn't trust him one little bit. "I can do it."

"Yes, but I don't want to just hand you a knife that you can use on me."

"Who says I don't have a dozen already strapped to my person?"

To be fair, she hadn't arrived armed, even though normally she didn't go anywhere without at least four blades and a gun. She hadn't thought it would send the right message. Besides, all killing Trick would do was transfer his blood-slave contracts onto his heir, whoever that happened to be. And Dru, his former assassin, didn't know the identity of the Halcyon Guild's beneficiary.

Since the heir was an unknown, Seraphina wasn't about to take the risk that whoever inherited the Halcyon Guild could be *worse* than Trick.

"You don't have any weapons on you at the moment, I know."

How he knows, that's the interesting question, she thought. *Although, I am a weapon myself. Best he not forget that.*

"Well then, by all means." She placed her hand in his, fighting back a surprised gasp at the heat that emanated from him. He was like a mini-inferno.

With a methodical slice, he cut open the skin on the side of her thumb. He then turned her hand, so that the blood ran down the digit, dripping onto the floor.

"Press this against the contract, next to Z's."

Following the direction, she left a bloody thumbprint right beside her fellow Dart's. The only difference, she was willing, whereas Z's print had been made when he was unconscious. Picking up the pen, she then signed her name next to the fingerprint, for added surety.

"Unnecessary, but okay, let's go with it." Trick rolled up the parchment, before it vanished into thin air.

Handy trick. She grimaced at her inadvertent pun.

"Now the kiss. It won't be so bad; I even brushed my teeth this morning." He grinned, exposing pearly whites without a single coffee stain.

"You demand a kiss to seal the deal with everyone you enslave?" How many people were in the guild, anyway?

"Only the special ones."

"Females, you mean."

"Come now, don't be so narrow-minded. Females, males, non-gender-specific individuals. Whoever tickles my fancy."

Narrow-minded? *Her*?

She'd never judged a person for their sexual orientation, skin color or species—aside from demons, but that was an angel's *job*. *I am not a bigot*. But back in Heaven, she hadn't really known anyone who wasn't straight or non-cisgendered.

"Apologies." She bowed her head ever-so-slightly.

Trick appeared startled at her response. Then he clapped his hands together, the momentary surprise gone. "Shall we get this show on the road?"

"Yes." Better to get it over with. "But I hope you don't expect me to pay off my debt on my back."

"No. Your talents are better suited elsewhere." He laughed, the sound rich and decadent.

Her stomach dropped. Someone as morally repugnant as Trick shouldn't be able to make such a melodic and wonderful noise.

The distance between them seemed to vanish, and Trick was barely a hair's breadth away. Since she'd fallen, Seraphina had kissed and been kissed numerous times. Soon after arriving in the Human Realm, she'd worked out that people were drawn to her looks the way bees were to honey. Her appearance had become a new kind of weapon; sex had simply been a new way to fight. But she'd never been nervous before, not until now.

Trick's lips met hers, the contact searing in its intensity. His breath tasted of mint leaves. His tongue tickled the seam of her lips, and she opened, dueling with him, refusing to submit. She would never surrender to anyone again—not a boss, a lover, or even a slave master. Her body and her mind were her own, and she would not put someone else's happiness above hers.

Soon though, the kiss deepened, grew hotter, sexier. Trick pressing his body flush against hers, the hard muscles of his torso meeting her breasts, which grew heavy and ached.

No. This is just business.

But she couldn't deny that her body wanted to rub against him, to feel the heat of his shaft pressed against her stomach. Her blood flowed hotter, thicker, and her fingers itched to trace over the bare skin of his body. Would it be as soft as it looked?

She had had numerous partners since her fall. None had tasted as appealing as Trick.

His hand slid down over her back, around to her hip, his fingers tightening over the curve. Then, all of a sudden, he broke away, placing several feet of distance between them.

"There, the deal has been sealed." He rubbed a hand over the back of his mouth, like he was wiping away the taste of her. Strangely, she didn't feel insulted. In fact, she wondered if he had done it to erase her taste, because it had been too good. Too delicious.

Like he had been.

No.

His wasn't the kind of kiss that left her craving more.

Definitely not.

But she knew it for a lie, even if she hadn't said it aloud.

A tingling sensation swept over Seraphina's lips, then they burned. Raising a hand to her mouth, she placed her cool palm against her lips, but it offered little relief. Thirty seconds later, the pain faded, as if it had never been.

He branded me there.

If she ever ran away or disappeared, he'd be able to track her with it.

The bastard.

But then, should she expect more from the leader of a mercenary guild?

You run one yourself.

Yes, and if her guild had slaves, she might have done the same thing, damn it.

It was a great way to mess with a new slave's mind, to keep them on their toes, to know that wherever they went, whoever they kissed afterward, they had their master's brand right there the whole time.

CHAPTER 5

That had been a bloody stupid idea.

Trick's cock still throbbed. He hadn't expected—or wanted—this erection. Even worse, Seraphina had kissed him with such ferocious control; she hadn't lost her head to lust at all. Cool, calm, methodical; it had fucking sent him wild. It was only when his hand had reached her hip that he'd realized she'd been playing him. No woman with eyes like hers melted for a man she didn't like.

For a man like *Trick*.

He'd almost been fool enough to fall for it.

Time to get your head in the game. No more weakness. No more pity. He'd taken Z on because he felt sorry for him, and look where that had got him. Into a huge fucking mess, where he was now lumped with some kind of damn valkyrie.

Back to business.

"Get your things and come back to the guild." Trick waved his hand dismissively. "We'll set you up with a room and work out what your first job will be."

Something far, far away from him.

Seraphina stared down her nose at him for a few seconds, then nodded, turned on her heel, and left.

The silence after her departure was deafening.

He strode back to the other side of his desk and collapsed in his chair. Rubbing a hand over his face, he exhaled slowly, trying to re-arrange his scattered thoughts. Kissing an angel was stupid—kissing Seraphina even more so. But he'd wanted to know what Heaven tasted like, just for a moment, before it would be forever out of his reach.

Amazing, he thought. *It had tasted amazing.*

He caught up with Dru in the stone-lined hall. She'd been waiting for him after Seraphina had vanished. "You didn't bring your guard dog with you?" he asked, looking for the hulking angel who had attached himself to Dru's side.

She gave him a flat stare. "If you mean Az, no. He's back in the Human Realm. Why? You fancy him?"

Trick rolled his eyes. "You know well and good it was you I wanted to fuck. Not some pretty angel-boy."

So. Seraphina knew Z, and Z knew both Az and Seraphina. Clearly, they'd all been buddies back in Heaven. Wasn't that great?

Now this asshole Az was Dru's mate, when Trick had spent years wanting her, willing to take the risk of dying in her arms. Except now when he thought of kissing her— like he'd done every day since he'd met her—it was no longer her mouth that Trick imagined. His mind conjured a set of plush, dark plum-colored lips, ripe for the taking.

This isn't good.

The idea behind the slave-branding was that *she* wouldn't forget *him*. Not the other way around. But the tart and sugary taste of ambrosia lingering on his tongue made it a tad difficult.

Stop by the mess hall and get a Coke or something. That would wash away the flavor. And he could do with the sugar hit.

"Come now." Dru patted his arm, pulling him from his thoughts. "We both know you had a crush on me purely because I was unobtainable."

"So was your sister, but I didn't want to bang her."

That comment earned him a dark stare before Dru walked back toward the main hall, the flickering lights sending shadows dancing across the fine contours of her face.

The thing was, Peony looked almost *exactly* like Dru — from the white-blonde hair, to the gray eyes and the golden skin. The only differences between the twins were their personalities and their ability to kill: Peony could do it with a single touch, whereas Dru had to use her claws. But no matter their similarities, he had never felt the slightest pulse of attraction to the guild's former medic. He'd just wanted the assassin. Which had told him it wasn't simply a physical thing.

He hadn't wanted a healer; he'd wanted a killer.

"What the fuck were you thinking?" Dru demanded when he caught up. "Sending Peony to the Mortus. She could have died."

"She didn't. And she's their goddamned queen now, so I think it worked out pretty well, don't you?"

It had been one of his luckier moments, that was for

sure. He'd taken a gamble and won.

If he'd sent Dru to the den, it's likely she too would have killed the king, but would have walked away afterward, leaving a high body count and the Mortus in turmoil. They would have eventually hunted her down, and then there would have been a bloodbath.

Peony, however, tried to see the best in people, and was compassionate enough that she'd want to help the demons she lived with, even if they were evil. Trick had figured she had a chance of surviving, at least. He hadn't expected her to thrive.

"I still want to kill you for it." Dru stopped walking. "She's trapped there, you know that?"

He frowned. "She's their queen, she can do whatever she fucking wants."

"She's been bound to Hell. She can't leave. At least not yet."

Bound to Hell?

He rubbed his chin. "Sorry to hear that, but it's not like anyone could have predicted that would happen."

Only the Hell-lords were bound to their realms. How on earth had Peony managed such a feat? Although...the power she would have gained from doing it...

A little shiver ran down his spine.

Better that he avoid her for the next hundred years or so.

At least.

"Are you done chastising me?" he asked.

She growled under her breath. "For now."

The admission made him grin. She'd forgiven him—at least a little bit. And that was a good thing, because while he had lusted after her enough to earn himself a reputation as a love-sick puppy, he'd valued her dry wit and friendship more. It was the latter he'd missed most since she'd left him.

Uh, left the guild.

"Good." He nodded. "Let's go get a drink while we wait for Seraphina. I have some gossip to fill you in on."

She rolled her eyes. "You know I don't listen to gossip."

"No, you just make it."

A deep, throaty laugh filled the hallway, making him smile. Dru wasn't prone to mirth, so he gave himself a mental pat on the back.

"Anyway, it's about Sylvester. He's gone and hooked up with someone."

Their resident thief, Sylvester, was also their current—and reluctant—medic, since it had proven rather difficult to recruit demon healers. Turns out, there weren't too many of them around.

Her eyebrows rose. "Really? Do tell."

"Oh, I'd love to."

For now, despite the shittest month in recent memory, everything was back to where it should be.

And he was happy.

CHAPTER 6

"Are you sure you need to leave?" Yael asked, for the tenth time in the past hour.

Seraphina glared at her fellow Dart while she packed a suitcase full of clothing. Her other case was already full of weapons. She hadn't been able to fit the rocket launcher, but she figured Trick would have one if she needed it.

She glanced up. "My answer has not changed in the past ten minutes."

"We will find another way around the contract—" Yael paced her bedroom, striding from one rose-gold-painted wall to the other.

"How? Are you willing to sign your soul over to the guild?"

Yael's mouth snapped shut.

As I'd thought.

Seraphina focused on the space around her. She'd miss this room, she supposed. It wasn't the first one she'd claimed at the mansion; she'd abandoned that after Paschar's visit. She couldn't handle sleeping in the place where he had betrayed her. But this space Seraphina had made her own—from the paint color to the carpet, it was lush warm tones, highlighted with aquamarine throw cushions and bedspread.

"If it was the only option available to us, I would have signed my name," Yael said eventually.

That took a little too long.

She shook her head, and reached for another shirt, this one the color of sunflowers.

Seraphina had done what needed to be done. She'd sold her soul, so that Z could remain free. He'd had enough bad luck in his life, and now that he was healthy again, he deserved a second chance. What's more, as the keeper of a piece of Heaven's Heart, it was better that he wasn't enslaved to a guild of mercenaries, who would use him for it the moment they knew.

Trick wasn't above using someone for his gain—look what he'd done to Dru's sister.

Thinking of Trick made Seraphina's lips throb. Repressing the scorching memory of his kiss, she firmly shoved a shirt into her suitcase. *It's just a physical reaction. It means nothing.*

"Surely—" Yael began.

Raze strode into the room. "Enough."

Thank you. She sent the thought to the other Dart, who briefly bobbed his head in acknowledgement.

"But—"

Raze crossed his arms over his chest. "Yael, we have spent over two weeks trying to think of a loophole; this is it. Badgering Seraphina for her sacrifice will not make it go away."

"But that's what I am saying. She doesn't have to make

a sacrifice at all if we think a bit more."

"It has already been done," she said.

Yael's head whipped around. *"What?"*

"I signed the contract two hours ago. This is not preparatory packing, this is me leaving."

"But we hadn't decided—"

"You hadn't. And we're done discussing this." In Heaven, Yael had been assertive and to the point, and always ready with a joke, but since their fall, he'd become arrogant and kind of rude. She wasn't sure if he'd always had those traits and just suppressed them, or if this was a new development. Either way, she didn't answer to him.

She never had.

"Fine." Yael strode out of the room, his mouth set in a thin line of anger.

Raze placed a gentle hand on her shoulder. "He feels guilty."

"He's hot tempered," she replied, shoving the last item of clothing into her suitcase. She'd left her Prada, Saint Laurent and Versace gowns behind. She doubted she'd have the space—or proper storage facilities—for them. And it wasn't like she was going to have to win clients over now; that would be Trick's job.

She'd just be weapon that delivered the death blow.

She was okay with that.

Killing demons is what I was born to do. What difference does it make if I get paid to do it or not?

Money, after all, paid the bills. And in this case, earned her freedom.

Ten million dollars. That's what Z was bought for. A pittance, really. But Raze can't buy the debt off, I have to earn it.

And most assassination jobs didn't pay that well—not for demons, anyway.

"I'd ask you if you were certain this is the right course of action, but you have already made up your mind." Raze stepped aside as she dumped her suitcase on the floor.

"A decision had to be made."

And she didn't have much to lose by making it. Only Raze knew about Paschar, and he wasn't going to tell anyone. Even if she got back into Heaven—if they managed to find all three pieces of the Heart—her name had been sullied. Her life as she'd once known it was over. It was better to embrace her future, no matter how bleak. Being an assassin wasn't too different from being a soldier.

Probably.

Possibly.

Maybe?

"You could have waited and discussed it with us first." Raze's reprimand was gentle, but she flinched nonetheless. He'd been Dina's second-in-command back in Heaven, and she'd always valued his opinion.

First Yael, now Raze. The only one who hadn't scolded her yet was Azrael, but he was off in Hell with Dru, doing God-knew-what.

"I discussed it with Z," Seraphina said. "His thoughts were what mattered."

The other angel had been fully prepared to sacrifice his future and happiness and go back to Trick, to earn off his debt. But that had been stupid, and Seraphina had been more than happy to point that out. It hadn't taken a lot of persuasion to get him to agree; he wanted to stay with Peony—the Mortus queen and his lover.

"It is done now," Raze said. "If you need our help, don't hesitate to ask."

The corner of her mouth turned upward. "We work for rival guilds now. That would be bad business."

He shook his head, storm-colored eyes serious. "I would never put business before friendship."

She allowed a full smile to bloom. "How did you get so filthy rich, then?"

"I am neither friends with the stock market nor the dead."

"I'll accept that. I had better get moving." She picked up both cases.

"So soon?"

"I need to stop by a store on the way and grab some supplies."

Raze pulled her forward into a hug, trapping her arms by her sides, the suitcases banging into her legs. "Take care of yourself. Don't lower yourself because you don't feel worthy. Don't let that asshole win."

She pulled away from the embrace. "I won't."

Seraphina knew that Raze wasn't talking about Trick. He meant Paschar.

"You're back!" The statement was made with the same amount of glee as if the speaker were a miner and Seraphina a brick of gold. Considering Dora Broome had made an obscene amount of money from Seraphina the last time they'd done business, the analogy was probably close to the truth.

Seraphina swept out a hand, taking in the whole magic shop. "How could I stay away?"

The store was cluttered with knick-knacks, candles, crystals, and containers. Floor-to-ceiling shelves lined the walls, while small tables and chests of drawers were scattered throughout the room, turning it into a small labyrinth. A stand next to her advertised 'The *real* way to detox', with a cluster of what looked like teabags perched in a copper bowl.

"I am going to ignore that sarcasm. And you don't want that tea unless you want a case of diarrhea to remember." A short, elderly human, Dora was remarkably spry and nimble for her age. She was also a witch Crone, and owner of Cat on a Broomstick, the best magical goods store in northern America.

"Who says it was sarcasm?"

The store *was* fascinating to Seraphina. On her first visit here, she'd been impatient and worried about Z, but she'd seen the results of witchcraft and knew that some humans had powers to rival angels and powerful demons. And this place was a hub of information about human magic.

Dora stopped a few feet away from her and tilted her head to the side like a bird. She rubbed her eyes. "That's a whopper of a brand. Wait a minute." She dug around in her dress—which had a surprising number of pockets—and pulled out a pair of sunglasses. Popping them on her nose, she smacked her lips together. "That's better."

"That's better?" Seraphina echoed.

"It was blinding me. Whoever gave you that kiss has a bit of juice." Dora's eyebrows waggled over the bridge of her glasses. She then grabbed Seraphina's arm and drew her deeper into the store.

"Funny you should say that," Seraphina muttered. "That's exactly what I've come to talk to you about."

CHAPTER 7

Trick wondered how long it would take Seraphina to set her affairs in order. *Hopefully a few days.* That kiss had left his lips stinging and his body primed for sex, which was unfortunate, because he wasn't about to get any, not anytime soon.

Sleeping with Seraphina was a *terrible* idea.

Too bad his mind had stuck on the thought.

Back in his office, he quickly checked his email, scanning through the job listings: 'Cleaner wanted for Spora demon'; 'Elimination of cambion requested'; 'DEATH TO ALL HEATHENS'. Out of interest, he clicked on the cambion message, since until a week or so ago he had employed three. Now he only had one.

Samuel McCoy?

Trick didn't know the guy. Delete.

He might run a guild chock-full of killers, but he didn't believe in picking on the weak or those just trying to get by. Most cambions were targeted because of their genealogy, not because of anything they'd done. It's why he'd bought Dru and Sylvester. The fact he'd taken a chance on them in a world that hated them, made them more loyal to him than the average employee.

Dru hates you now.

To be fair, he wasn't sure how much she'd liked him to begin with. That's what made her moving in with her angel-boy lover all the more unbelievable. She hadn't given Trick a chance, and she'd known him for decades. Then she'd met that Az guy a couple weeks ago and suddenly it was time for Happily Ever After.

He's her mate.

Yeah, well, that changed things up a bit.

Anyway, it's time for you to move on. Stop being bitter. Life's too short and all that.

In his case, life was too long for that. He already held one mammoth grudge, and he didn't have room for any more.

Suddenly, there was a low chime, like the tinkling of bells, and his skin itched.

Someone was trying to teleport in.

Lowering the wards around his office with a clap of his hands, he kept his face blank as his guest appeared in front of him.

The visitor had an enormous body, ebony-dark skin glinting blue in his office's lighting, and splayed wings with feathers as white as snow, threaded with thick veins of gold.

An archangel.

What. The. Actual. Fuck?

Leaning back, Trick kicked his feet up on his desk, clasping his hands behind his head.

The angel's upper lip lifted in a sneer. "Guild master."

He smiled. "Uriel."

Heaven currently had fourteen archangels. Over the millennia, there had been more, and there had been less, but for the past four thousand years, it had been fourteen. Hell, on the other hand, had three Hell-lords, followed by numerous demon-lords, dukes, and 'custodians'.

Trick, however, was a force of nature all on his lonesome. And he didn't answer to Heaven's enforcers.

"That's Archangel, to you," Uriel snapped.

Trick opened his arms wide, in a mockery of welcome. "Come now, your reign of terror does not extend here."

"'Reign of terror?' Trust you to see it that way. We are doing God's will." Uriel looked as if he were about to spit on the floor, but caught the icy glint in Trick's gaze and seemed to reconsider.

Trick might not be an archangel, or even a Great Duke, but he wasn't weak, and had the power of a thriving guild behind him.

"So why do you dare to enter Hades' realm, Uriel?" He rested his hands on his stomach.

Uriel glanced around, as if searching for a place to sit. When no such comfort appeared, the angel widened his stance, and put his hands behind his back, military-style. "It has come to our attention that you have enslaved one of our kind."

So. They had finally heard about Z.

He'd had the angel in his possession for weeks—why come to him *now*?

The thing with angels—they could sense lies. So, he had to be careful with his phrasing. "I do have an angel blood-slave, that is correct."

Uriel's dark eyes flashed, illuminating the room with an arcane glow. "How *dare* you!"

Trick kept his face bland. "He was sold to me. And in rather poor condition, I might add. So really, the blame is on you."

"On *me?*" The glow faded, probably more from surprise than anything. Uriel wasn't the kind of being who was used to having people defy him.

"You're the archangel. Why'd you let a baby angel get abducted and then tortured? Surely you and your brethren were powerful enough to make sure that didn't happen."

Uriel's irritation was palpable, but his words were calm. "Zadkiel was a fully-fledged soldier. He was well able to take care of himself. You have much to answer for."

Ire, pure and unholy poured through Trick. "I don't have to answer to you. Ever. You are in *my* guild, in Tartarus, a realm that has nothing to do with you. I purchased Z in good faith, and you are the ones who failed to prevent demons from raiding Heaven and losing him in the first place. You failed. The *archangels* failed. And you blamed some poor group of angels for it. Those schmucks were nothing but scapegoats. All of Hell can see it, even if your angels can't."

When the other mercenary guilds had finally realized who exactly ruled the Falling Star, it had been the talk of the three circles of Hell. But business was business, and despite the gossip, or perhaps because of it, the Falling Star was still approached for work.

"They were an elite unit trained to protect Heaven's Heart. They failed, and the Heart was stolen." Uriel's lips thinned.

Trick's pulse accelerated briefly before he wrested it

under control. Heaven had lost one of its most treasured artifacts?

Not my business.

"That's unfortunate."

"*Unfortunate?*"

"Look, you aren't here to talk to me about the Heart. Unless you want to hire the guild to find it for you?" Trick quirked an eyebrow.

Uriel's face pinched. "No."

"Then why *are* you here?"

"You are going to sell Zadkiel back to us."

"I am going to do no such thing."

"What?"

"I am not going to sell Z to you."

"But—you must."

"No, I really mustn't."

Surprise, shock and anger warred for supremacy on Uriel's face. Did he think he could just waltz into Trick's office and he would just roll over and beg for orders?

Probably. Uriel is one of the more arrogant archangels.

They should have sent Aurora or Michael for this. Or even Gabriel. Uriel was too much of an ass for Trick to want to help him.

"The only offer I would accept is like for like. Do you have an angel you would be willing to trade for Z?"

Guile flashed in dark eyes. "It could be arranged."

"You wouldn't offer yourself?"

"Don't be ridiculous." Uriel shook his head, as if the concept of signing his soul away was beyond sense. "If we get you the angel, will you give us Zadkiel?"

A direct question. One he couldn't lie to. "No."

"Then what was the point of asking us about the

trade?"

"I just wanted to see how sincere you were."

"You waste my time."

Like Trick gave a fuck about Uriel's schedule. "If you want Z to return to Heaven, you can ask him yourself."

"But your slave contract—"

"No longer applies to Z. Another angel traded her life for his."

Silence. Then, "Who?"

"Seraphina. You may not understand loyalty, but she does." And it was a trait of hers he could admire.

"Fine. I will find Z and ask him. Where is he?"

Trick laughed. "As if I would tell you. Now get out, my patience wears thin."

"*Your* patience?"

Trick snapped his fingers and Uriel vanished.

The surprise on the archangel's face as he disappeared was priceless; a memory to treasure.

Whistling, Trick stood and walked over to his door. Time to go back to the main hall. He gave the doorframe an affectionate pat on the way out.

That was the thing with wards created by Hades himself; they were powerful enough to eject even an archangel.

CHAPTER 8

Seraphina's new chamber was small to the point of being tiny. Compared to her room back at the mansion, it was the size of a broom closet. Trick had clearly given it to her as a statement of her importance to the guild—it signified her lack of it.

But this room, with its single bed, desk and bathroom, was bigger than the space she had called her own in Heaven. Luxury was something she had only come to appreciate after her fall.

I did without before, I can easily do so again.

Although, she would miss the small haven she had built for herself at Raze's. The bare walls and cold stone floor of this room lacked the warmth and vibrancy of her red-gold chambers. *You're in Hell, what did you expect?*

She dumped her suitcases on the skinny bed—*lucky I don't have wings anymore; I wouldn't fit on it otherwise*—and then turned to Trick, who was leaning against the door jamb, arms folded loosely over his chest.

"Does this meet with your approval?" he drawled, brown eyes glinting with amusement.

"It's fine." She didn't plan on being here for decades, anyway. The sooner she worked off her debt, the better.

"I'm sure it's not what you're accustomed to."

Something shimmered in her peripheral vision and she moved to examine it.

Glitter?

A small pile of it had gathered in the corner of the room and she dabbed a finger into it. Holding it up to the light, she frowned. Then she looked over at the other corners—more heaps.

"An anti-listening spell." Trick's deep voice rumbled in her ear.

Startled, she whipped her head toward him. He was barely a foot away.

He moves silently for someone his size.

Don't be stupid. He runs a guild of assassins. He would have to have learned a trick or two about staying undetected.

There it was again—trick.

Ugh.

"Looks like someone didn't want you listening in to their conversation." She dusted her finger off, but all that seemed to do was rub the glitter over her other fingers and hand.

Trick shook his head, a mocking smile on his lips. "Don't bother. It's permanent."

Quick as a snake, she darted her hand out and wiped the glitter over his face.

There. Now he sparkled like a vampire from the *Twilight* series.

"What the fuck—"

"You're welcome!" She gave him a sunny smile.

He glowered, brown eyes fierce in a face marked by shimmering flecks of gold. It actually made him more handsome. Her smile died.

Trick rubbed a sleeve over his face, then cursed when it came away covered in sparkles. "I am going to give you the worst mission I can think of."

"I did you a favor. It suits you."

He held his arm away from his body, as if it were diseased. "I never took you for a smartass."

"Your mistake." She'd never been quite so verbally combative before. She'd certainly never been that way with Paschar. She'd often had the urge to be cheeky with him, but had doubted his ability to understand the humor. He had always been so serious, so intense. Fun with him hadn't really been a thing.

It floored her to realize that.

And to realize she found Trick...amusing.

He was a jerk, sure. Self-centered. Arrogant. And morally reprehensible. He *owned* people's souls. But despite his irritation at having glitter rubbed over him, he hadn't told her off, he hadn't thrown a mantrum. He'd just...dealt with it. Paschar would have been furious with her and no doubt lectured her on her maturity and the dignity of her position in Heaven.

Why the comparison? You aren't in a relationship with Trick.

No, and she had no intention of changing that.

Trick stared at her, and she forced herself to hold her place. She would not be intimidated by him. Her skin warmed as the room built with electricity, with...tension.

Suddenly, the air burst with an audible pop, and a new figure appeared next to her desk, behind Trick.

Relief almost made her sag.

It hadn't been sexual tension that she'd been reacting to, it had been an incoming teleporter.

Seraphina reached for a dagger before she remembered they were in all her suitcase.

You need to have a weapon on you at all times.

Power radiated from the stranger in a blast, sizzling along her skin. He was enormous, his body boasting muscle upon muscle, and his yellow eyes were like jewel chips. His jet-black hair was French-braided down the middle, and shaved on either side, making him look like a badass. But the kicker? He was more handsome than almost any man she'd ever seen—except maybe Trick. Oh, the new guy had all classic lines and beauty, but it was topped with a ragged kind of charm. Although, his jeans and T-shirt combination seemed to somehow make him more...approachable.

Who is he?

Trick spun around, then raised an eyebrow at the intruder. "Hades, how good of you to drop in."

Hades?

This was the Hell-lord who ruled Tartarus?

He wasn't what she'd expected.

But then, she wasn't sure what she had thought he'd look like. A deposed god, formerly a chthonic deity; she figured he'd be pallid, a smidgen on the thin side.

She hadn't thought he'd look like sex-on-a-stick.

"I like to keep my finger on the pulse, you know?" The god's voice was deep and gravelly, and horribly provocative. Quite different to Trick's bedroom-smooth tones.

You really have fallen, to find a former god attractive on any level.

At the same time, she had a pulse. *Anyone* with eyes in their head would find Hades handsome.

"Is that intended to be ironic?" Trick asked.

"I always intend to be ironic." Hades' expression was deadpan, so Seraphina wasn't sure if the sarcasm was deliberate or not.

"Isn't it Asha's job to do these drop-ins?"

"She's on holiday."

"Holiday?"

"Yeah. You know, off exploring the great outdoors, seeking revenge on enemies, sunbathing, that kind of shit."

Trick put his hands in his pockets. "Got it."

"Who's Asha?" Seraphina asked.

"My PA," Hades said, then focused on Trick. "Okay. I have three questions. One: why do you have a fallen angel with you?"

Trick flicked her a glance. "She's my newest blood slave."

"Huh." Hades' lemon-yellow eyes surveyed her from head to toe. "At least she's pretty."

What the Hell?

"Two," the god held up another finger, "why the *fuck* was an archangel here?"

Shock turned her limbs to lead. An archangel had been here?

For me?

No. That was foolish. If they'd wanted to come for her, they could have done so at any time before now. But what had they wanted from *Trick*?

"Uriel paid me a little visit," Trick replied.

"No doubt because you've got a fucking angel on the payroll now."

"No doubt."

Hades glowered. "I don't like angels—no offense, sweetcakes," he nodded at her, "—and Uriel fucking broke protocol by entering my realm without talking to me first. They stop by again, you call me. Got it?"

Sweetcakes?

"Got it." Trick gave a short nod.

Hades' expression was of tightly controlled rage. He looked like he wanted to pace, but took one step before he realized he had nowhere to go. "Why the Hell are you in this room, anyway?"

"Is that your third question?" Trick asked.

Hades' eyebrows lowered into a frown. "No, it's a goddamn bonus."

"I was showing Seraphina her new room. Welcoming her to the guild family, et cetera, et cetera."

"Right." Hades' gaze flicked to her. "Word of advice, angel, if you want to get back into Heaven, don't do the horizontal tango with him, you get my meaning?"

"I get it. And why would I?" She tossed her hair over her shoulder.

Trick placed a hand over his heart and winced. *Theatrical fool...* But she had to fight to keep the smile from her face.

"There's a bed here, and your slave brand is on your lips, so..."

"Can everyone see that?"

Trick shrugged. "Those who can see magic, sure."

She pointed a finger at him. "You little—"

"Anyway." Hades clapped his hands. "I still have to

ask my third question."

"Fire away," Trick said.

"Okay. Last question—and the most important one." Hades paused for effect. Seraphina leaned forward in anticipation despite herself.

"Why the fuck is there glitter all over your face?"

CHAPTER 9

Great.

Even Hades was laughing at him now.

Trick fought the urge to rub his nose, knowing it would only spread the irritating sparkles everywhere. Who would have thought that Seraphina had a sense of humor?

Not me.

She'd struck him as the serious type from the moment he'd seen her, when she'd first started making public appearances for the Falling Star guild. Serious, sensuous and sinister. The kind of package he normally went for, provided it was demonic in origin. He didn't do angels.

But now he'd kissed her?

He just wanted *more*.

Which was insane.

"I may have wiped glitter on him," Seraphina admitted, holding up shimmering hands.

Hades shook his head. "The leader of an assassination guild who looks like he's got more in common with Edward Cullen than Vlad the Impaler. They just don't make them like they used to."

"Edward who?" Trick asked.

"Gods, read a book." Hades rolled his eyes.

Seems like I need to expand my information quest. Trick valued intel like some people valued breathing.

"Now, let's go somewhere more comfortable," Hades said. "This room makes me feel enormous." He clapped his hands, and a breath later, they were in a large stone chamber, with a high gothic-style ceiling, stone floor and walls, and an expanse that was punctuated by gargoyles.

Trick swallowed.

He'd heard of this cavernous space before. It was the Hall of Statues—and despite its lack of imaginative naming, the place was seriously fucked-up.

A warm cloth appeared in Trick's palms, and he stared at it blankly.

Hades waved a hand. "Wash your face."

Right. He scrubbed hard at his cheeks and, lo and behold, the cloth came away glittering with tiny flecks of gold. "Does this actually get it off?"

"Sure does."

"You need to sell them. You'd make a fucking fortune." The material disappeared from Trick's hands before he could pocket it. "I'll buy shares."

"Uh, can I have one, too?" Seraphina asked.

Hades frowned at her. "I'd say no, but I don't want glitter all over my shit."

Soon after, the fallen angel was industriously cleaning her hands. Her cloth did a disappearing act, too.

"Now, I have a mission for you both."

"For us *both*?" Trick asked. Hades didn't normally bother to get involved in the guild's business. When he wanted someone eliminated, he sent an email or a text message like anyone else. The fact they'd been brought here meant it was personal.

This is not good.

Gods—even deposed ones—had a way of ruining people's lives.

Trick didn't need his ruined again.

"Yes. Only a *true* fallen angel can take care of this for me." Hades' gaze bored into Trick before focusing on Seraphina with interest. "And look what we have here."

"*An angel?*" Seraphina bit her lip. The magical mark blazed at the contact.

I really shouldn't have done that.

Whatever. Trick could change the mark's location, although that would mean touching Seraphina again, and he wasn't sure that was a good idea.

He might not want to stop, next time.

There will be no 'next time'.

"A *true* fallen angel. And I just happen to have one right here." Hades smiled, but his eyes remained cold and calculating.

"What do you need a fallen angel for?"

"I need one to retrieve an artifact for me." The god clasped his hands behind his back.

"Retrieve or steal?" Trick asked, not that either option really bothered him. When it came to ancient objects, they had usually been stolen by their current owners anyway.

"Either," Hades answered.

Seraphina snorted. "You're a god, can't you do it?"

Trick winced. He was going to have to have a talk to her about the importance of not pissing off Hades. She might have been an angel, but the man before them had always been a god. They had never been—and never would be, unless she ascended to archangel—on the same playing field when it came to power.

But Hades surprised him by not smiting her. "I'm not a fallen angel, so no."

"But—"

"Sweetcakes, I rule Tartarus. I referee souls. I don't have time to go running around trying to find knick-knacks. But I'm rich as that fucker Croesus used to be, so I pay people to do it for me. That's where you come in."

"I see."

"You'd better. You're new, and you're about to work for me, so I'll give you some slack. But be warned; I have no patience for people who annoy me." He looked meaningfully around the hall.

Seraphina's chocolate-hued gaze followed, confusion marring her face.

Trick decided to fill in the blank. "All these statues are people who angered Hades."

Every gargoyle here was a demon or human who had gotten on the wrong side of the god and been magically transformed into a stone figure, placed here for eternity. Or until Hades forgave them.

And Trick had never heard of anyone being forgiven.

Her eyes widened. "You can turn people into stone?"

"Clearly." Hades waved a hand in the air.

Her lips compressed into a thin line.

Maybe she had finally realized that she was in over her head.

Yeah, I doubt that.

Trick had the feeling she never thought *anything* was too hard for her to achieve. Which wasn't a bad thing, he realized. He was much the same. Hell, he'd carved a new life out for himself, and had been kicking goals ever since.

"So, what's this mysterious artifact?" Trick asked. He leaned forward, trying to work out what the gargoyle closest to him had been before its transformation. Possibly a Yolar demon? They had four genders, and delicate pointed features that reminded him of the legends of the Sidhe.

"It's called the *Amenonuhoko*." The name rolled off Hades' tongue with perfect intonation. *Japanese*. That was about as much as Trick could ascertain.

"The amen-what?" He rubbed his jaw.

"The *Amenonuhoko*. Translated, it means the 'Heavenly Jeweled Spear'."

You could have led with the English version. But whatever. A name was a name.

"What does it do?" Seraphina asked.

Trick sighed. "It doesn't matter what it does. We steal it for Hades, we get paid, that's how it works."

Hades laughed, the sound booming around the room. "I knew there was a reason I liked you, notwithstanding your enslaving of angels." He clapped Trick on the back, the force almost knocking him off-balance, and Trick was no lightweight.

That guy is way too strong.

The god turned his attention to Seraphina. "The *Amenonuhoko* was used to create *Onogoro-shima*, a primordial landmass. The spear was given to two gods by primordial deities. It is a tool of power. You want to know more, Google it. I'm not your fucking encyclopedia."

A primordial artifact.

There had once been many; now there were just a few left in the world. Most had been locked away by ancient gods, afraid that they would be used against them. Odin's Orb, which Trick had hoped to steal a mere month ago, was one such artifact. Heaven's Heart was another. Legend had it that the Heart had been broken into three parts to prevent it being used by the wrong hands. Two of those pieces had been missing for millennia.

Trick had a habit of keeping up to date on legends—you never knew when they'd become profitable—but he'd never heard of the Heavenly Jeweled Spear.

The HJS. There, that was better. He couldn't be bothered saying the full name every time.

Seraphina frowned. "But why can only a fallen angel touch it?"

"Only a fallen angel can *retrieve* it," Hades said.

"But—"

The god sighed. "Lucy—I mean, Lucifer—stole it a thousand years ago. To prevent the rightful owners from stealing it back, he put a spell on it."

Of course, he did.

Nothing was ever easy.

"Only a true fallen angel can remove it from its protective casing," Hades said.

"So, we just need to go to Sheol and get it back?"

"That's the thing. I have spies in Lucy's main residence, and they say it isn't there. So, if he's got it, it's not in his Tower of Tortures."

Lucifer's name for his Sheol residence.

It does sound more menacing in ancient angelic.

"So, when do you need it by?" Trick asked. "And have you hired anyone else?"

"There aren't too many fallen angels around, you know? They have a habit of dying in Hell."

That didn't really answer his question.

Hades raised his hands, as if he was about to clap them. "Oh, and you have a week to find it. If you fail, you die. Gotta run. Errands and shit."

There was a boom, and they were back in Seraphina's room, Hades nowhere in sight.

Great. A week to find it, or we're both *dead.*

"Can he do that?" Seraphina asked, shock lining her face.

"Yes."

Trick answered to Hades, that was how being a guild-owner in Tartarus worked. But the god had never pulled rank before; he'd let Trick run his business autonomously. To force Trick into this job meant that the god *really* wanted that spear.

What else can it do?

"Does he mean it? If we don't find this artifact, then we're both dead?"

"That's what he said." But Trick would read the contract that was no doubt waiting in his inbox, to make sure those were the true conditions. Not that Trick could negotiate; Hades' will, was, well, Hades' will.

Seraphina sat on the narrow steel-framed bed, her head hanging low for a few heartbeats. Her dejected appearance tugged something in the vicinity of his heart.

Don't be stupid.

Then her head rose, and she met his stare with furious determination. "We'd better get started then. I have *no* intention of dying by *your* side."

Ouch.

But whose side *was* she willing to die next to?

CHAPTER 10

One week.

That was practically no time at all to find an ancient artifact that Lucifer had been keeping hidden for a millennium. Where could Seraphina even start to look? Nibbling her lip, she mentally flicked through a list of contacts she had developed since falling to the Human Realm. There were communications managers at other mercenary firms, and a few high-powered demons, but none with the kind of intimate knowledge that could get her details on Lucifer's stronghold.

The Tower of Tortures.

She shook her head at the name.

Pacing her tiny room, she twirled a dagger she'd grabbed from her suitcase—the blade's movements helped soothe her, so she could concentrate.

"You could poke someone's eye out with that."

She came to a sudden stop, peering over her shoulder at Trick, who stood in the doorway. In his hands he had a small box, wrapped in brown paper and tied up with a twine bow.

He's giving me a gift?

A thrill of excitement shot through her, before she managed to wrangle the emotion under control. *Don't be ridiculous. It's not a present. And it's probably not even for you.*

"Here. This is for you."

Tentatively, she reached out to take the package, knife still held tightly in her left hand.

"Hell, it's not a box of herpes. Take it." He shoved it at her. "Some old woman came here, hit on me, and left it behind. Said it was for you."

Relief swamped her. It wasn't a present. Eagerly now, she grabbed the box and tore off the paper.

There. It was perfect.

"Lipstick?" Trick asked, glancing down at the small tube in her hand.

"Yes." She removed the lid, idly taking note of the color: bright, cherry red. She'd asked for a clear lip gloss, but clearly Dora had other ideas.

She could almost hear the Crone's cackle as she ran the lipstick over her lips. Her mouth burned, as if she'd been stung by a bee, then went numb.

"What kind of lipstick is *that*?"

Trick was staring at her mouth.

"Designer."

Designed to hide your slave-mark.

His eyes narrowed. "Hmph."

She was surprised that he let it go so easily.

For now.

He would no doubt bring it up later.

Time to change the subject. "Why are you here?"

He strode further into the room, and sat on the edge

of her desk, looking as comfortable as if he were in a recliner. "Oh, did you miss the whole you-will-die-in-a-week-if-you-don't-get-the-HJS-thing?"

"The HJS?"

"The *Amenonuhoko*. Heavenly Jeweled Spear. You know, the thing that Lucifer stole, and we have to find?"

"Yes," she ground out. "I just hadn't realized you'd already given it an acronym."

She wanted to smack the smugness from his face.

I will not *die next to this man.*

Seraphina had sold her soul to save Z. She wasn't going to waste it.

"I am all about efficiency." He flicked out a hand. "Now, we need to find out which stronghold Lucifer has stashed this artifact at. Any ideas?"

"Oh, yes. Let me just check the list of his properties I have on hand." She rolled her eyes.

"Sarcasm, while generally a very useful thing, is not useful now."

"I was just trying to think of any contacts I might have who would know about Lucifer. But I didn't really come into contact with anyone who worked closely with him. Have you done any work for a Great Duke of his?"

Each circle of Hell was run independently of the other. Hades ran his like the very profitable business it was. Satan ran his through coercion and greed, with demons often enslaved to do his bidding. Lucifer had a collection of lords and ladies, with his Great Dukes the generals of his vast army and empire.

Trick nodded to himself. "I know of a former Great Duke."

Surprise lanced through her. "You do?"

"Honey, I know a lot of things. I collect information like some people hoard treasure."

"*Honey?*"

"You're right. It doesn't work. I'll think of another nickname."

"*Nickname?*"

"Seraphina is such a mouthful. Can I call you Sera?"

"No."

"Good, I'll stick with that for now. But I will think of something else, don't worry." He patted her shoulder as he walked back to the door.

"Where are you going?"

"To call the Great Duke. Are you coming or not?"

She grabbed the knife's sheath from the bed and strapped it on. "Do I need to lock the door?"

"I would." He tossed her a key.

She quickly locked up, then followed him down the hall. "Why can't you just call him now?"

"I need someone to give me his private number."

They emerged into a large chamber with three hearths, a long table, and a gaudy golden throne.

Is this Trick's throne room?

The seat itself might have been called opulent, if not for the sheer brazenness of its design. It reminded her of rich old ladies who wore their entire jewelry collection in one go, to show off their wealth.

Trick nodded to the series of demons who were scattered around the room; some on sofas in front of the fireplaces, others at the long bench, and some milling in dark corners. He came to a stop next to a lithe, handsome male demon, with chestnut-colored hair and baby-blue eyes. He was handsome, in a GQ-model kind of way.

He's not as attractive as Trick.

No. She did *not* just think that.

"Sylvester." Trick clapped the demon on the shoulder, oblivious to Seraphina's internal horror.

"Boss." He nodded his head at her. "Stranger."

"I'm Seraphina." She stuck her right hand out, and the demon stared at it for a few seconds before shaking it in a firm grip.

But he withdrew his hand quickly before turning to Trick. "Fallen angel. *Another one.*"

So, he'd known about Z. And from the disapproving tone, he hadn't been happy about it.

"She traded her soul for his. What could I do?" Trick held his hands out, palms up.

"Right. So, he's no longer on the look-for list?"

"Oh yeah, I should cancel that." Trick whipped out his phone, fingers flying across the screen as he typed rapidly. "Sent. Thanks for the reminder."

She could get whiplash from the speed at which he changed tack.

Sylvester spun away on his heel. "Anytime. Now, I've gotta run. Got a date—"

"About that..." Trick said.

"About my date?" Sylvester pivoted back toward them.

Trick flashed him a charming smile. "Could I get his number?"

"No." Sylvester crossed his arms over his chest. "He's mated. To me."

"Oh, not for sex. Even though we know he'd totally want me." Sylvester glowered at him. "If he was single."

"Then why do you want his number?"

"I need to chat to him about Lucifer."

Challenge sprung to life in Sylvester's blue eyes. "Why would he know anything about Lucifer?"

He's very combative for a slave.

Did Trick allow all his blood slaves to talk to him like that?

He lets you.

Maybe Trick was more relaxed than she'd thought?

"Want me to spell out that answer?" Trick asked.

"Fine. Come with me. But the angel stays here."

Trick shook his head. "No can do."

"She's a hindrance."

"True. But Hades gave her and me a mission, unfortunately. We have to do this together. So, she comes with."

She was both insulted and pleased by Trick's response. Sure, he had ridiculed her—again—but he was willing to work with her to achieve their goal. He could have snuck away and done this behind her back, calling her in at the last minute. He didn't have to include her. She was only required for the final retrieval.

Sylvester sighed. "I'll text you the address. Meet me there."

"Can't I just call him?"

"No."

"Why not?"

"Phones can be traced."

Then the demon strode out the hall, leaving Trick to check his phone.

"Do we follow him?" she asked.

"No." He took hold of her hand and she gasped slightly at the heat of the joining. Warmth radiated up her arm, pooling low in her stomach.

A breath later, they were standing beside a sleek pool, the water a clear crystal blue. In front of them perched a glass-walled house of elegant, modern architectural design, complete with polished concrete floors and industrial lights. The backyard edged onto a forest, and the air was crisp and cool with only a hint of pollution.

Whoever lives here has money. Lots of it.

Inside the house, Sylvester emerged into the main living area, a male of similar height by his side. Human? Demon?

Probably demon.

The doors opened and a blast of power hit her with physical force, but she gritted her teeth and stood her ground.

Demon. Definitely demon.

The figure beside Sylvester was dressed in an immaculately tailored suit—probably a Burberry—with a white cotton shirt, and highly polished Guccis. Dark red hair was swept back from his widow's peak, and he surveyed them with hard brown eyes. The only thing that marred his appearance was a series of faint scars on one cheek, crisscrossing lines that made his handsomeness brutal in its intensity.

"You wanted to meet me?" the stranger asked, his voice gravelly, liked he'd smoked a cigar a day for a century, or he'd roughened it through screaming.

"You're not a Murmur demon." Trick's voice was accusatory, but it just made the powerful demon smile.

"Oh, I'm a Murmur all right."

Her eyes widened at the admission. Murmur demons could control a person's thoughts; they could make a person hand over millions in cash, fall in love, or even kill themselves. After the Mortus and Infernus, his species were perhaps the most feared.

"Don't worry," he said to Seraphina. "Most angels are immune to a Murmur's talents."

That's what they said in Heaven, but she couldn't bring herself to be relieved just yet. She'd learned that what Heaven said and what actually happened were two different things.

Blasphemy.

Maybe. But she wasn't a blinkered fool anymore, to believe that what everyone told her was fact.

Lies, she'd found, could be disguised as truth.

"I love your strength, your loyalty, and your beauty," Paschar had said.

Not, "I love you."

He hadn't been lying, and she had elaborated the rest. She should have realized then that Paschar's motives weren't pure, but she'd been so in love, so willing to overlook his faults, that she was blind to the reality of their relationship.

No longer, she thought. *No longer will I blindly accept another's word.*

No.

Next time she fell in love—if she ever did again—it would be because she was *shown*, not told, that she was valued, cared for and loved.

CHAPTER 11

Trick tried to ignore Seraphina's sudden melancholy. Why was she sad? Was she thinking of Heaven again?

You're meant to be ignoring her.

Right.

Easier said than done, apparently.

But he had to get his head back in the game. The demon before him was no ordinary Murmur and Trick didn't like the fact Sylvester had been keeping secrets.

"Why do you have the power of a god?" Trick asked.

Sylvester flashed the demon-slash-god a sharp glance. "I thought you were cloaked," he muttered.

"Some people can see or feel power, no matter the glamour," the god whispered back.

And Trick was one of them.

Trick had sent the cambion to do a protection job—something that Sylvester didn't particularly enjoy doing—and Sylvester had ended up nearly dead, and mated to one of the most powerful demons in the Human Realm. Or Hell.

Trick was *not* jealous that Sylvester had found his one

and only.

Plus, Trick had thought they were friends, but the debrief Sylvester had given Trick had missed the fact that Mr. Daemon—CEO of the Three Circles Recruitment Agency—was a fucking god.

"A god?" Seraphina's clear voice rang out. "I thought there were only a handful left."

"More than you'd think, less than you'd credit," Mr. Daemon said.

"That's a non-answer if ever I've heard one."

The former Murmur demon tilted his head to one side. "I was once a god, once a Great Duke to Lucifer, and now the CEO of a demon recruitment agency. Is that enough information for you?"

"But gods aren't allowed to run those," Seraphina said.

And it was true.

A deal had been struck between the three Hell-lords—demons needed access to humans, but humans were supposedly protected by Heaven. Seven agencies were established to enable demons to infiltrate human society in secret, where they could act on their baser urges discreetly. However, they had to pass the agencies' tests to see if they were suitable for resettlement, or work in another circle of Hell.

As the position of CEO came with a significant amount of power, no god was allowed to fill the role. The Great Culling had resulted in the majority of ancient deities being deposed and killed—both Heaven *and* Hell liked it that way. So, there was no way a god should have been able to rise to CEO.

"I gave up my godhood to take on the role. But I

almost died recently, and that broke the chain on my power. I don't have to give it up a second time." The grin on the god's face was wolfish.

"How can you be a demon *and* a god?" Trick asked.

"How can you be a jerk and a douche?" Sylvester muttered.

Mr. Daemon raised an eyebrow. "One parent was a Murmur, one parent was a primordial deity."

Trick kept his expression neutral, but inside, he simmered. He'd considered Sylvester a friend, as much as a person could in a den of assassins. But now, both he and Dru had shown that Trick wasn't as valued in their opinions. Dru, he could understand. But Sylvester?

"I would have charged you more, had I known," he muttered. And he'd already charged the demon a fortune. "Anyway, Mr. Daemon, we're here to ask you some questions as a former Great Duke."

Seraphina mouthed 'Mr. Daemon' incredulously.

Yeah, it's not the best pseudonym.

The god must have caught Seraphina's expression. "Call me Laird."

"Laird? As in *Lord*?" Trick asked.

"As in Lord."

Hrm. A number of gods had 'lord' in their names. Lord of the Mountain, Lord of the Earth, Great Lord... Hell, the angels' man-up-in-the-sky liked to be called that.

But Mr. Daemon did not strike him as an Indian deity, nor a Gaelic one, nor a Mesopotamian one...he didn't have their power signature, for starters.

His magic didn't remind Trick of Hades, so he ruled out Greek out, along with Roman...

Levantine? Or maybe Persian...definitely *not* Egyptian...

"I can *see* you thinking," Sylvester said.

"There are a lot of gods to sort through."

"You are trying to work out his god-name *now*?"

"When else would I do it?" he muttered.

"Back when you had access to a library?" Seraphina suggested.

Which, sure, was logical, but he kept information stored in his brain like it was a library anyway.

"I can feel his power right now, which makes working this out easier," Trick said. "And I've met gods of varying religions before. I assume he picked 'Laird' because it's a loose translation of his actual name. The fact he picked a Scottish word is deliberately done as a red herring. He isn't a Gaelic god. So, I can rule that out. While a lot of Hindu gods have 'lord' in their title, he isn't of the Indian subcontinent. He could be Norse, but they have a particular feel to them—they're salty. Briny. He's not of the Asian continent, either. Their gods tended to have the appearance of their people. And I've met an Asian deity before."

Asha Himm, Hades' personal assistant, was a demi-goddess at the *very* least. Not that Trick let on he knew; she was trying to keep it a secret. Said she was a cambion, of all things.

"So that leaves the Americas, the Pacific, the Near East, and Africa. But again, I think I can narrow it down to the Near East. For some reason, those deities managed to survive the Great Culling more than others."

"Cut to the chase, Boss." Sylvester sighed.

"Baal. You were Baal." As soon as he said the name, it

fit.

Both of Laird's eyebrows rose, and then he barked out a laugh. "For centuries, no one even suspected. And yet you guess right in a matter of minutes."

"It wasn't a guess."

He collected information for a reason.

"God of Thunder?" Seraphina asked.

"Storms," Baal—Laird—corrected. "And fertility."

He used to spend time in the Underworld.

The fact he was half-Murmur made a Hell of a lot of sense now. The time he was down in Hell meant he was away from the Human Realm and its denizens. It—

"Now you have sorted out my god-name, what do you want to know about my time as a Great Duke? It was more honorific before the Culling, more practical after."

"We need to know about *Amenonuhoko.*"

"The Heavenly Jeweled Spear?" Laird asked.

"You've heard of it?" Seraphina asked.

"It was one of Lucifer's most prized possessions. Why?"

"We've been asked to retrieve it."

Laird's eyes narrowed. "I am not going to help you steal from Lucifer. He may not be my liege anymore, but I am not about to cross him, either."

"We just need to know where it is."

The god shook his head. "I haven't been a member of Lucifer's household for a thousand years. The last time I saw it, it was at the Tower of Tortures, but he moves his artifacts around a lot. He likes to travel his kingdom, never spending too long in one place, even his stronghold."

"Can you tell us the locations of his other houses?"

Trick asked.

"The information is a millennium out of date."

"Better that than nothing."

"It will cost you."

"I have money."

"Oh, I wasn't thinking cash." The god flicked his glaze to Sylvester, then back to Trick.

"I am open to negotiating."

I have no choice.

Thanks a lot, Hades.

CHAPTER 12

Seraphina's cellphone was ringing when she returned to her rooms. Trick had dropped her off before heading to his office to start negotiating with the god. She didn't mind that he was excluding her from that; the Halcyon Guild was Trick's business, not hers.

She picked up her phone as the call went to message bank. With a frown, she saw that whoever it was hadn't left a voicemail, but had rung several times already.

She sighed as she called the number back.

"It's about time you returned my call." The speaker sounded annoyed, their voice crackled with age.

"Dora?" Seraphina asked.

"The one and only."

"This isn't your normal number."

"No, it's a burner phone."

"Why are you using one of those?"

"You're in Hell. I don't want people tracking our communications. Witches are meant to be neutral."

"You mean they're meant to work for the highest bidder."

"Exactly. Neutral. We go where the money is; we don't care if it comes from angelic, demonic or human hands."

Seraphina laughed.

At least the Crone was honest.

"Why are you calling me?" she asked. "Didn't the payment for the lipstick go through?"

That little tube had cost more than her Jimmy Choos.

"Sure did."

"Then why chase me?"

"A little birdie told me you're on the hunt for a magical artifact."

Shock sizzled through her. "How did you hear that?"

"I am not the Crone of Crones just because I look the part."

"Why call me if you know so much?"

"You have money, and I have information. I like to make money, and I am sure you like intel."

Could she trust the tiny human?

Sure, they had successfully done business together a number of times now —and Seraphina had an internal lie-detector. But witches, she'd learned, were sneaky.

Go with your gut.

And her gut said to pay Dora a visit.

"Okay. Let's meet. But if you're selling me bogus info, you will have to refund me. And I'll leave a bad review online."

"You're harsh, angelcakes."

Angelcakes?

It was so close to Hades' fake endearment that she could guess the identity of the Crone's 'little birdie'.

"I can one-star you all day, if I need to. When do you want to meet?"

"Now is a good time. Oh, and one thing..."

Seraphina was already digging through her bag, checking to see if she'd packed a Devilsgate spell. She could ask Trick to teleport her there, but he was busy, and she wanted to keep Dora as an ace up her sleeve.

He took you with him. He shared.

She wasn't about to play fair with a demon. If this panned out, she'd tell him, then. She wasn't as trusting as she'd once been.

"What?" Seraphina asked, when Dora didn't elaborate.

"My granddaughter doesn't believe in magic. So, keep the angels and demon talk to a minimum, *capiche*?"

There it is! She grabbed the spell, and another two daggers.

Then Dora's words registered. How could the granddaughter of the most powerful witch in all the Americas not believe in magic?

"*Capiche.*"

The Cat on a Broomstick had a little back room that Seraphina had never seen before. It was a stark contrast to the front of the store: this space had little clutter, and contained a sofa, table, chairs, and refrigerator. Not a single shelf or jar of suspicious-looking powder was in sight.

"I thought I said to keep the angel crap to a minimum?" Dora grumped, stomping into the room.

"I haven't *said* anything." Seraphina held up her hands. And she couldn't help being an angel, fallen or not.

"You used a Devilsgate to get here."

"I did it in the back alley." She'd figured that was less likely to be seen by humans. Or Dora's granddaughter.

"She was just taking the trash out. She could have spotted you."

"But she didn't. So, it's fine."

The old woman glared, her eyes pools of darkness in the electric light. Power clung to the Dora's skin, like she had given up trying to hide it from her. Could other people sense it?

"Why doesn't she know, anyway?" Seraphina asked, taking a seat on the cream-colored sofa.

"We tried to show her when she was younger, but she didn't believe it. She has no active magic of her own. Witch magic isn't all sparkly lights and glittering spells, like with demons. It's subtler. So, she thought we were making it up." The Crone limped over to sit next to Seraphina on the sofa. "After a while, she convinced herself the stories we told her were just make-believe, and that the shop is just catering to pagan humans who are delusional about the world."

Seraphina winced in sympathy. "But if she saw our magic..."

"Then she would probably have a seizure. She appears to be fundamentally incapable of believing in what she can't see or do herself. And I don't want to force it on her. The majority of humans have no idea that demons and angels exist, so the family decided to let her be like them."

"But you used her back at the mansion, for Z. Or was that another granddaughter?"

Dora had done some astounding healing magic back

at Raze's, when they'd first found Z. But she'd needed more magic than her body could contain by itself. As a result of that encounter, Seraphina had been forced to accept that some humans were powers to be reckoned with, rather than just ignored.

"It was the same granddaughter. She's a conduit. I just told her to go and meditate somewhere and be 'open'. She thinks I'm nuts when I ask for her to do it, but I say it helps convince clients that we're actually doing the job. She doesn't argue about money."

"She thinks you're a charlatan."

"Yes."

"That's got to hurt."

A shrug. "I've grown used to it."

"So, what's this information I need to know?"

"Don't want to negotiate the price first?"

"I can't tell how valuable it is until I hear what you have to say."

The Crone sighed. "Fine. You're looking for the Heavenly Jeweled Spear. It was stolen from its last owner by Lucifer."

"I know all that."

"But did you know that he put a spell on it by which only a true fallen angel can take it from its case?"

"Yes."

"Do you know what it looks like?" Dora smirked.

"No."

"That's where I can help you. Well, sort of. My granddaughter can fill in those blanks."

"But you said she doesn't believe in magic."

"She doesn't. But she's an archaeologist, and she'll be able to help us."

"I thought she worked here."

"On weekends, to help out her poor old gran." Dora flashed a toothy smile.

"Because you're so feeble," Seraphina murmured.

"Delicate as a flower," Dora agreed, chuckling.

CHAPTER 13

Seraphina watched as Dora whipped out her phone and punched the surface a few times with her index finger. Soon after, the door opened, and a pretty redheaded woman poked her head inside the small back room.

"Gran? Do you need anything?" Keen green eyes surveyed the area, landing on Seraphina with caution.

"Rowan, please come in."

"No one will be out front, then." The woman stood halfway in the doorway and glanced almost longingly over her shoulder.

"Your cousin will be here any second. Ah, there he is." Dora smiled as a bell chimed in the store.

Rowan peered back into the shop, then nodded. She closed the door behind her with a sigh. "What do you need me for, Gran?"

The human—witch—was tall and lithe, with skin the classic pearl-white of a redhead. Her jeans and green tank spoke of a practical nature, but she had tiny little beaded pins in her hair. Purely decorative.

Layered, this human is layered.

And apparently close-minded.

"I have a client here who would like to know more about an ancient artifact," Dora said slowly.

Rowan's jade eyes narrowed. "What kind of artifact? You know I don't want to have anything to do with the antiquities market. It's corrupt, and it's destroying archaeological sites quicker than I burn in the sun."

"It's not for sale on any antiquities market," the Crone said.

That we know about.

She should research that. The information could very well have an asking price in Hell, especially if Hades had more than one team on the job.

"Oh." Rowan eyed Seraphina suspiciously.

Is it because I look corrupt?

Hell couldn't have affected her so quickly. She'd only been there a matter of hours. But she *had* been in the Human World for almost seven months. It had changed her somewhat, that she could readily admit.

Rowan walked toward them, then leaned down and whispered in the Crone's ear. "Your rich clients always want something they can't have."

Lucky Seraphina's hearing was much, much better than any human's—or witch's.

At least the human didn't trust her because she was rich, not for any other reason. *If I deteriorate too much more, the archangels won't accept me back, no matter if we find all three pieces of the Heart.*

And she had to get back into Heaven.

It was where she belonged, no matter that her name was worth less than mud right now.

I will repair the damage that Paschar did.

"Seraphina here just wants information," Dora said, drawing her away from her spiraling thoughts.

"I am after an accurate description or image of an artifact known as the *Amenonuhoko*." Or the HJS, as Trick called it.

She fought back a smile.

He really did make her want to laugh, and there was nothing wrong with honest laughter; the Lord knew, she needed it.

"It sounds Japanese," Rowan said, straightening. She strode over to the small table, grabbed a chair and sat down. "My specialty is Egyptian archaeology, specifically, the Old Kingdom. I only have a passing familiarity with East Asian history."

"You have access to books, though," Dora said. "And other archaeologists."

"I guess I could ask some of my colleagues at the university." Rowan nibbled on her lip as she thought, but didn't sound enthusiastic at the idea.

You don't need enthusiasm. You just need action.

Funny, how that mental voice sounded so much like Dina.

There's a black-winged angel in Hell.

Could it be her?

It has to be. Unless there are more fallen angels than the archangels admitted. There was Lucifer himself, Paschar's brother—Cassiel, Florian, Muriel...she counted up to two dozen that she was aware of.

It could be anyone of them.

But we lose our wings when we fall.

The only two that hadn't were Z and Dina, because technically they hadn't fallen.

Rowan withdrew her phone from her jeans pocket and typed madly on the screen. Then she read, "Otherwise known as the Heavenly Jeweled Spear, it was used to create the primordial land-mass *Onogoro-shima*. It is sacred to the Shinto religion." She looked up at them. "This is a legend. An origin story. It's not a real artifact."

Right. She doesn't believe in magic.

If she did, she'd know that there was truth behind every legend.

Seraphina cleared her throat. "I have information that indicates a replica was made in ancient times." She may be able to sense a lie, but it didn't prevent her from telling one, although it did leave a sour taste in her mouth.

"If it was made in ancient times, then that makes it an artifact. What do you want with it?" Rowan crossed her arms over her chest.

"I believe it has been stolen."

"And why would you want to find it?" Suspicion laced her words.

"To return it." Again, a lie.

"The original owner would be long dead."

Possibly. Or maybe not. It depended on whether that owner had been human or not.

"Their family won't be."

She was going to need to eat a mint after this.

Rowan settled back. "If it's real, you need to hand it back to the people."

"Rowan! We do not dictate to our clients," Dora chided.

Fire flashed in Rowan's eyes. "I did not spend seven years at university, and become a *doctor*, to help people steal artifacts!"

"You're a doctor as well?" Seraphina asked. She thought it would have taken longer than that to become qualified in two such diverse fields.

"I have a PhD in archaeology."

"Oh, so not a *real* doctor, then."

Rowan glared.

Seraphina saw Dora suppress a smile.

"I am not interested in thievery," Seraphina said, flicking her hand dismissively. *Truth.* "I just want a description of the spear so I can help locate it."

Also truth.

She was beginning to understand how easily Paschar was able to hide his true motivations. A little bit of truth here, a little there, and let the recipient fill in the rest.

"Rowan—" Dora began.

"Fine. I'll make some calls. Come back in a week." The redhead made to stand.

"No good," Seraphina said, shaking her head. "That is too long. I need the information now."

"I said a week."

"And I said that's no good. I need it by tomorrow."

"Tomorrow?" Disbelief flashed across Rowan's face. "It's the weekend."

"So?"

"So, people don't work on the weekend."

She looked down at herself, then at Rowan. "I am. You are."

"I'm helping Gran out."

"I am working," Dora pointed out.

Rowan groaned. "Fine, I'll make some calls today. And I'll go the library tomorrow. Okay, Gran?"

"Why can't you go to the library today? What if you

need to go to more than one?"

"Fine! I'll go now." With an annoyed glare, Rowan stormed from the office.

"How old is she?" Seraphina asked.

"Almost thirty."

"A baby, then." That explained the tempestuousness.

"By your standards, I guess she is. By ours, she's an adult. I apologize for that display. She has become cantankerous of late."

"Her temper is of no consequence." Working with demons had taught her the real definition of temper tantrum. "Do you think she will be able to find something?"

"Rowan has a...knack for finding the almost impossible. She won't credit it herself, but she has found everything I have ever asked for."

"Magic?"

Dora nodded. "Quite possibly a latent ability."

"A handy person to know," Seraphina murmured.

"If only she believed in magic."

CHAPTER 14

Trick scowled at Baal. He couldn't think of the god as Laird, even though he was trying to. Names were important, after all. Chosen ones especially so. But Laird just didn't suit the guy. Baal did.

"I am not going to give you shares in the guild." Trick shook his head. He could see where this was going.

Come in hard, then pretend to settle.

It was one of his preferred negotiating skills. Less so when it was used *against* him.

"I need to get something out of this. If I give you information that leads you to the artifact, and Lucifer discovers it came from me..."

Baal tapped a long elegant finger on Trick's desk, which was covered in paperwork.

"You're untouchable, you know that. Besides, what if your information is useless?" he asked. "This deal will only work if you give me something that directly leads to the prize."

"That is too subjective." Baal shifted on his chair. When it had become apparent that Trick wasn't about to bring a seat for the god to sit on, he'd simply teleported in his own, despite Trick's wards.

That said a lot about the deity's power.

Trick was expecting another visit from Hades as a result.

So he can give me another impossible task to achieve.

He liked deadlines, but one week?

Only six days left. They were three-quarters through day one already.

"You don't *need* shares in my business," Trick said.

"I don't *need* anything. But Satan found a loophole in the contract regarding my role—and its level of associated protection—a bare month ago and hired three guilds to attack me. If not for Sylvester, I would be dead right now."

"And you got Sylvester through me. As part of a favor to Hades. Remember that." Normally, Trick would have kept well away from a job that involved another Hell-lord, but Hades had asked ever-so-nicely—that's to say, he'd demanded it. "Plus, word is that the loophole has been sewn up."

"That one has, yes."

"As if you didn't get any others fixed in the meantime. The six other CEOs would have been throwing money at their lawyers as well. They would have been sweating bricks at seeing you attacked."

The CEOs of the recruitment agencies were meant to be exempt from Hell's politics, and untouchable by the three Hell-lords, unless they broke their own contracts, which Baal hadn't done. He'd simply arranged for Asha Himm to be employed by Hades. Satan hadn't been happy about that arrangement, and had spent ten years plotting revenge.

That had all been in the debrief.

Damn Sylvester and his selective sharing.

Trick grabbed a pen, then tapped it against the papers. "You want Sylvester to have shares in the guild."

Surprise surged in Baal's eyes before vanishing again, buried away. "You assume much."

"I am currently on a deadline, I have a guild to run, a fallen angel to manage, and I haven't eaten in a good eight hours, apart from some scotch and a couple of pieces of candy." Trick dropped his pen. "I don't have time to be given the runaround. Do you want the shares in Sylvester's name or not?"

"Yes, I want them in his name." Baal sighed. "You like to suck the joy out of life, don't you?"

"Yeah, I should have been a lawyer."

Baal laughed, but sobered quickly. "Thirty percent."

"No fucking way. Five."

"*Five?*"

"This is a flourishing business. And being a guild master comes with certain...perks. I am not going to just hand over my hard work for a little piece of information that may nor may not be helpful."

"Thirty."

"Five."

He wasn't about to budge on this. Enslaving souls in Hell gave a person power. The more slaves, the more power. Trick could teleport, cast his own spells and heal from almost all wounds; he was a hair's breadth from being classified as a sorcerer. It was why he preferred to enslave rather than employ, even though he treated all his blood slaves as if they were employees. He let them have their free will, even if it cost him, like it had with Dru. And many of them stayed on as actual employees when their contracts expired. If they survived to the end of them, anyway. Assassination was a risky business.

"How about you text Sylvester and ask him what he would settle for?"

"I don't need to text him." Baal sniffed.

Right. Murmur demon. They had the whole telepathy thing going.

It was a good thing Trick had a natural shield.

"He says thirty percent."

But Trick knew Baal was lying. Smiling, he whipped out his cell and dialed. "Sylvester. Just the man I wanted to talk to."

❉

Trick was scraping the last piece of steamed tapioca pudding off his plate when Seraphina found him. Annoyance tinged her expression, but she was still breathtakingly beautiful. Unfortunately. His fingers itched to trace over the midnight darkness of her skin.

Errant, Trick's sex-addicted demon administration officer, paused in his recap of the guild's current finances. He stared at the fallen angel with a slightly open jaw. "She really *is* an angel."

"What? You thought I made that part up?" Trick asked.

"Shut your mouth, Errant, or you'll start drooling." Opal, a Radiato demon and assassin, slapped Trick's bookkeeper on the shoulder. Errant jerked forward, almost face-planting into his untouched serving of pudding. Despite her skeletal appearance, Opal was strong.

"Are you going to eat that?" Trick pointed his spoon at the bowl. Monica—a Foraci demon with exceptional culinary skills—was on cooking duty and he had a closet sweet-tooth.

Errant scowled. "It is filled with tiny eyeballs. Or eggs. I have yet to determine which."

Tiny eye—

"They are tapioca pearls." He held out a hand. "Give it to me."

"They are *pearls*?" Errant held the bowl up to his face. "Why did you let Monica raid the treasury to make a dessert? I will have to add this to this month's outgoings..."

Trick ran a hand over his face.

Really?

Seraphina's low, sensuous laugh wove through the room. She sat down at the table with her own bowl of pudding. "They are not real pearls. They are starch balls."

"Starch? As in a carbohydrate?" Metcalf, the guild's only Reynard's Imp, had arrived. The small gray-skinned demon was vicious, psychotic, and had a problem with vegetables—like they were a personal affront to his character. He'd also been avoiding Trick since Peony's departure. The imp had valued her as a friend. Go figure.

Then again, the imp liked Sylvester, and they weren't exactly two peas in a pod, either.

"As in a carbohydrate," Seraphina replied. Trick couldn't gauge her reaction to the demons in the room, but she seemed unfazed by them.

Considering her former role in Heaven, this should

have been close to torture for her. There was a Foraci demon, a Renyard's Imp, a Pestula demon, and so many others that were classified as 'kill on sight' for angelic warriors. But there she was, eating her dessert with a look of amusement on her face.

At least she isn't annoyed anymore.

And thankfully she was wearing her lipstick again.

Some of the demons here, like Monica, could see magic, and would have noticed Seraphina's slave mark.

Really should have thought about that more.

Ah well. He'd just have to change it.

Even though it meant touching her.

That wouldn't be such a bad thing, would it?

Considering he'd vacillated from wanting to have his hands all over her, to not wanting to touch her at all—for the sake of his mental health—he figured it would be a bad thing.

"I really don't understand what you humanoid types see in carbs. Don't you know they go straight to your thighs?" Metcalf tapped his chin, his eyes narrowing as he considered Seraphina's bowl. "On second thoughts, keep eating them. More on your thighs means more on my dinner plate later."

A knife appeared suddenly under Metcalf's chin, Seraphina's hand steady as she held the blade out. "I will never be on anyone's dinner plate. Got it?"

She pushed the blade until blood seeped from a tiny wound.

The imp nodded, deliberately pushing the blade further into his skin. Rather than the rage Trick expected, Metcalf gave Seraphina a toothy smile. "Got it."

Fucking psycho.

But this episode reminded him that he had a little more paperwork to sort out after assigning Sylvester seven percent of the guild's shares.

He had a new heir to name; he refused to give Sylvester the entire business anymore.

Who will it be?

CHAPTER 15

Trick closed his MacBook with a click, and then sat back on his throne, throwing one leg over the armrest and leaving the computer lying against his belly. It was his usual pose; he thought it gave off a certain casual disrespect that he liked. Seraphina watched him with laser focus from a seat near one of the hearths, and he sent her a small mocking wave. She'd been staring at him for the past twenty minutes or so, trying to get his attention, but Trick had been busy working on Halcyon Guild admin duties; obligations that never seemed to end.

He was responsible for the lives of forty demons and one angel. Just because *his* life had a one-week expiry date, didn't mean that he was about to shirk his responsibility to his guild's members.

Don't go telling anyone that or they'll think you care.

His phone beeped and he fished it out of his pocket, juggling the MacBook in the process. It was from Sylvester and read: GOT IT. CHECK UR EMAIL. It was followed by an emoji of an eggplant and a smiling face with its tongue sticking out.

Ugh. Shortened text speak *and* emojis. Trick hated both, which is precisely why Sylvester would have used them. The guy just liked to irritate him. *At least he does know how to spell.* Some demons actually thought 'UR' was correct.

Why do I think of him as a friend, again?

Trick placed the cell on the throne's armrest, then opened his MacBook up again, giving a low whistle as he read the email.

Seraphina was by his side in an instant. "What is it? Is it related to our job?"

"Sure is," he replied, eyes skimming the text. He opened one of the attachments and grinned.

"Show me!" She reached over to grab the laptop, but he moved it away, lightning-fast.

"I don't think so."

"But it's about our job. You should share the information."

"Just like you told me about your trip to the Cat on a Broomstick? Plus, you didn't say the magic word."

"Your computer is locked with magic?"

"No, it's not locked with magic. You didn't say 'please'—that's the magic word." And he thought *his* knowledge of colloquialisms was subpar. She clearly had been living under a rock. *Her head has been in the clouds, literally.* Warrior angels would have had very little to do with humans and their sayings—they were trained to fight demons and only that. *So, she, at least, has an excuse. You don't. Your hatred of emojis blinds you to new information.*

A frown formed on her face. "Wait. You had me followed?"

"I don't need to." Trick ran a finger over his lips. "I have other means of knowing where you are."

Her eyes followed his movements. "You put a *tracking spell* on me?"

"Sure did."

"Do you do that with all your slaves?"

"No, you're special."

Since Z had vanished from his cell—and Trick hadn't been able to track him down using the angel's slave brand—he'd changed his policy on new slaves. Every new member of the Halcyon Guild would get a tracking spell along with their brand. He'd been complacent once before, never again.

Trick had thought that there was no way Z could escape; only three people knew of his location, and the angel had been so weak and emaciated from previous torture, he would never have made it out on his own. But Dru had somehow worked out where Z was and freed him the day she left.

How she'd gotten him out, Trick still didn't know.

I should ask her the next time I see her. He was still in the process of stitching up the security flaw. It wasn't like Dru had been on speaking terms with him until now.

And even if he hadn't decided it would be a good idea to track all his new slaves, he'd wanted a little extra information about Seraphina and her whereabouts. All he'd had to do was include a dash of additional magic in her brand and *voila!*, he could now track her whenever he wanted.

"Here, work out what the emojis mean. If you do that, I might let you see the email." He handed her his phone.

She took it and stared at the screen for a few moments,

frowning. She gave it back soon after, not even having tried to scroll up and read the previous messages between him and Sylvester, or sneak a look through other message windows. She earned some serious brownie points for that.

No. You're meant to be thinking of the bad things about her, not the good.

Right. He should make a list of the negatives, so he could focus on those, rather than wondering if she still tasted as amazing as before, and if her lips were really as soft as he remembered...

Bad things.

Right.

1. She doesn't know the magic word
2. She's too beautiful
3. She murders demons

He had a feeling that number three should really be in the number one position.

"I'll message Yael and ask him about the emojis."

She plucked her phone from her pocket and typed rapidly. It vibrated in response.

"That's cheating." An ugly green emotion rose in his gut. "Who's Yael?"

"He's another member of the Falling Star."

"Right." Another damned angel. And just because she knew him, it didn't mean they were sleeping together.

Not that it matters if they are.

"I think he's still mad at me," she said.

"Why would he be mad at you?" Trick asked. *Please do not be a lovers' quarrel.*

"For selling my soul to you."

"Oh, that. He needs to build a bridge."

"Why? Can you construct a bridge between the realms?"

"What? No. So he can get over it."

"Get over what?"

"Being angry."

"I don't understand how construction work will stop Yael being mad at me."

"It's metaphorical."

"Oh, I see. I hadn't heard that expression before."

I'm going to have to speak in simple language, he thought. At least for the next week or so. After that, they wouldn't be spending much time together, so it wouldn't matter.

"What did he say?" he asked.

"He said 'suck my dick'."

"He *what*?" Trick leaned over and grabbed Seraphina's phone.

"Hey!" But she didn't snatch it back.

The messages read: WHAT DOES AN EGGPLANT PICTURE, FOLLOWED BY A SMILING FACE POKING ITS TONGUE OUT MEAN?

It was followed simply by: SUCK MY DICK.

"I think that's the translation, not him being annoyed."

The contact in her phone had the name 'Yael', but the picture was that of a handsome cartoon character with jet black hair and pale blue eyes. Some popular culture thing. He would have to start watching more TV. With a quiet sigh, he handed Seraphina her cell back. His list of tasks was never finished.

"But what does an eggplant have to do with it?" she

asked, pocketing the cell.

"My guess is it's a substitute for 'dick'."

"Right. But why an eggplant?"

"I don't know. Google it."

"I just saw you work out which deity a Murmur demon was, and you don't know this?"

"Sugarpie, I don't make money from emojis, but I do from knowing who I am working with. It's called priorities."

"*Sugarpie*?"

"You're right. It doesn't fit." He shook his head sadly. "You're much too salty for that."

"*Salty*?"

He swore he could almost see steam pouring from her ears.

Trick turned back to his laptop. "So why were you at the Broomstick?"

"I'll tell you all about it if you tell me what your email says." Her lips flattened when he just stared at her. "Please."

"There! You're learning already. And who says you can't teach an old dog new tricks?"

"*Are you calling me a dog*?"

"Uh, no..." That was a bad idea. And he'd just decided he wouldn't do metaphors anymore.

"Guys! The boss just called the angel a bitch!" Metcalf screamed across the hall and then everyone was talking loudly, some laughing, some wondering when Trick was going to get castrated.

Banging my head against a brick wall would be more productive.

Seraphina sniffed.

Taking pity on her—and perhaps feeling a smidgen of guilt—he turned the screen toward her. "Sylvester emailed me a list of Lucifer's residences, and even included plans to five of the seven."

"No," the angel breathed, her eyes lighting up with excitement.

"Oh, yes."

She smiled at him, the expression making his breath seize in his throat. He didn't think he'd ever seen something so beautiful before. "We might survive the week."

He returned her expression, his sly. "We just might indeed."

If he didn't die of a heart attack first.

CHAPTER 16

Rowan Broome slammed her book shut with a sigh and rubbed her eyes. Her glass coffee table was scattered with volumes, the sheer number of red, green and blue tomes a testament to her speed-reading abilities. She'd rain-checked with her boyfriend Eric to spend time researching Japanese mythology, so that her Gran could coax her rich client into parting with her cash. Not the way she'd planned to spend her weekend.

Why did I let her talk me into this?

Because you're a soft touch, that's why. And you're an enabler.

Rowan's whole family was insane. Each and every one of them. They'd all swallowed Gran's nonsense that magic was real, and that she was some super-powerful Crone chosen by a council of equally deluded witches. And they treated Rowan like *she* was the mentally unstable one, because she didn't believe them.

The worst thing? She let them do it, because she loved them.

So much so that it was now three in the morning, and

she was rifling through her third library-book haul. She'd even spent a few hours searching journals online and reading some conspiracy theory websites, which had really just hurt her head and made her angry.

Aliens did not build the pyramids. God is not real. Curses can be explained.

Of course, her task would be much easier if she read Japanese.

Dr. Yamamoto had been as helpful as he could be at two on a Saturday afternoon, but he'd only read of the spear in passing. It was a legend, although he had spent a good fifteen minutes postulating which of Japan's numerous islands was the location for the sacred *Onogoro-shima*, the landmass that had supposedly been raised by the spear.

I wasn't asked to find an island.

That said, all of this research *had* made her want to read a bit further into the history of Japan. But that could wait. For now, she was just looking for references solely related to the description of the spear. So far, she had four photographs of paintings that she thought were reliable images of it. The majority of sources stated that the spear was a *naginata*, which was more like a pole weapon: a staff tipped with a wicked-looking blade.

You just want a replica. Not the real thing.

She was still leery of Gran's client, no matter that the woman was supposedly tracing the artifact for its real owners. *Individuals shouldn't own artifacts, anyway. They belong to the people, to the world.* But even Rowan could acknowledge there weren't enough museums to house all the artifacts in the world.

So, if she really *was* hunting down a stolen relic...

There was something almost...inhuman about the beautiful woman. In fact, Rowan didn't think she'd ever seen someone so attractive in all her life. Not even in the movies, or on TV. It was like she had been cast from a mold—from her perfectly spaced eyes, to her sharp cheekbones and her delicate jawline, she was physical perfection.

I wish I was even half as attractive.

And there it was. The little green monster she'd spent her entire life trying to exorcise. Jealously did no one any favors, and she shouldn't envy things that were completely out of her control. She looked how she looked—gangly limbs, fiery red hair, and freckles. So what, that she wasn't a classic beauty? She had her brain, and focus, and drive.

Rowan could achieve almost anything she wanted to.

Actually, I have seen people as attractive, she thought, picking up the next book. *Back at the mansion where the client lived.* Rowan had driven her gran there a few weeks ago so she could do some 'magic'. *More like smoke bombs and hand-waving.* There had been two other men there, both so handsome it had almost hurt her physically to see them.

And one of them had touched her.

Rubbing her left hand absently over her bicep, she sighed. Her arm had ached for a week after that. Not from a bruise or anything she could see, but something beneath the skin. It wasn't an injury; the guy hadn't even grabbed her too hard, just firmly. And she'd understood later why he'd manhandled her—he'd thought she'd been sent to spy on his house so it could be robbed. When you were as rich as they were, she could understand the fear of being burgled.

Maybe it hurt because your conscious was twinging. Because, for a moment, a brief flare of time, she'd totally forgotten she had a boyfriend she loved. She'd been so gobsmacked by the hazel-eyed man's beauty that she'd almost asked him out for a coffee, just so she could stare at him some more.

Reality had returned quick-smart, as had embarrassment and shame.

I am not a cheater.

Not that the guy would be interested in someone like her, anyway. He'd seemed more of a rough-and-tumble kind of man, and she was bookish and nerdy.

You love Eric.

Yes, she did. And one day, she'd marry him and maybe even have a kid or two with him. That's if she got tenure.

Her phone buzzed. It was Eric.

YOU UP?

YEP.

U SHOULD GO TO BED.

I WILL SOON. JUST FINISHING THIS JOB OFF FOR GRAN. WHY ARE YOU AWAKE?

WOKE UP & THOUGHT OF U. DON'T STAY UP MUCH LONGER.

I WON'T. LOVE YOU.

U 2. NITE.

She put her phone back on the table, a small smile on her lips, her heart full. Eric was everything she'd never known she'd needed: smart, sarcastic and funny. And another redhead.

Our future kids are doomed.

It was three-thirty now and she really needed some sleep.

One more book.

Pulling one toward her, she read its title: *A Catalogue of the Private Collection of Luke M. Starre.* Huh. How'd this end up in her pile? She must have grabbed it at random. Flicking through the pictures, she frowned at the photographs of delicate Ming vases, ushapti statues, canopic jars, and even sarcophagi of varying cultures.

Most of these would have come from the black market. Egypt, especially, did not sell its antiquities.

Then she froze as her fingers grazed a photograph of something that looked horribly like a *naginata*.

Frantically, her gaze raced toward the caption: *Purported replica of the* Amenonuhoko. There, in bold color, was a picture of a bladed staff, complete with a ring of delicate gemstones where wood met steel.

Surprise made her fingers clench on the book.

She'd found it.

Now, who is this Luke M. Starre?

CHAPTER 17

Five days left.

And, *of course*, Lucifer had seven strongholds scattered over Hell and the Human Realm. *He couldn't have just one or two*, Seraphina thought. He had to have *seven*. She ran her fingertips over the printed plans, flicking her eyes over the other papers. Her small desk could barely fit a third of the drawings. The rest were spread over her narrow bed.

Studying the plans of five of the residences made her head hurt. *So much to memorize.* She'd done it, but now her mind brimmed with hidden passageways and turrets, panic rooms and halls that she may never see in person. And who was to say that the layout was the same now as when the houses had been constructed? Laird had only been able to produce these plans from memory and hearsay.

"Want to come and hang out in my quarters?" Trick's voice broke through her concentration. He stood with one arm up against the door jamb, half-hanging into the room, and too handsome for his own good.

Too handsome for *her* good.

Her mind went blank for a moment, and her lips burned. "Uh, no."

"Not for *that*." He almost looked offended. *At her refusal, or that she'd thought that's what he had meant?*

She frowned. *You're the one who branded me on the lips.*

"What's so much better about your rooms than mine?" She waved a hand around the small chamber. She still had room to put things on the floor, if she needed it.

"One: space. And two: I have a cool spell that allows plans to be turned into three-dimensional models."

"Can't we do it here?"

"Too small."

"But I've already memorized them."

"Then you can help me do the same."

With a sigh, Seraphina stood and followed Trick out the door. They weaved through numerous corridors, passing a strange assortment of demons. Her time in the mess hall earlier had been illuminating, although her fingers had itched for her blades. Foraci demons were will-benders, akin to Murmur demons. And Radiato demons were so rare and deadly that they had a capture-on-sight standing order. And the imp had just oozed evil.

They are your comrades now.

Seraphina wanted to argue that, but she couldn't. She was a blood slave, and likely so were they. She might be forced into working with them on missions. She didn't want a blade in her back, so she had to get along with them, and she didn't want to cause the death of someone she was working with, either.

They are but pawns, as well.

Yes, but would her superior officers back in Heaven

be so understanding?

Paschar would kill them. She almost snorted at that thought. *Actually, Paschar wouldn't want to get his hands dirty.* He'd never wanted to spend time with her after a day's guard work, not unless she had already bathed and was neat and tidy.

He's not your problem anymore.

Too bad her heart hurt whenever she thought of him. *All those wasted years.*

Trick's rooms were located down a series of hallways close to the throne hall. She fought to keep her jaw from dropping at the sight of them. The place was like a small apartment all of its own, with living area, kitchenette, and doorways leading to other rooms, which she presumed included a bedroom and bathroom. But the living area was clean and elegant, except for the miscellaneous piles of magical items and technology scattered throughout. A series of red-gold paintings hung on the stark white walls, the splashes of color abstract in their detail, but beautiful, nonetheless.

"Where's this spell of yours?" Seraphina asked.

Trick closed the door behind her, then cleared the coffee table of everything except a small golden-flecked crystal. "This cost me a small fortune, but so worth it."

He rotated the crystal three times clockwise, twice counter-clockwise, and once clockwise.

She memorized the movements. "It doesn't turn on with an incantation?"

"No. The creator wanted it so that anyone could use it, regardless of language." He flicked her a mischievous glance. "Then again, it wasn't originally designed for enlarging blueprints of houses. But I like to consider myself an ideas man."

"So humble."

"Humility will get you killed."

Trick ran the crystal over a plan he'd unrolled, and a holographic image of the blueprint beamed into the air above the table. The three-dimensional map glittered with golden flecks. *It's beautiful.* And very detailed. Trick held a hand up to the image; with a swipe of his palm, the plan rotated.

She let out a low whistle. This *was* impressive. She'd never seen its like before.

Gabriel would have loved this.

Her former master was responsible for Heaven's security. He was also in charge of reconnaissance missions. This would have made things far easier for his scouts—of which she had been one.

"You look sad," Trick said suddenly, the plan glowing in the air between them.

"I'm fine."

"You're lying."

"Does the brand tell you that, too?"

"No, I'm just really good at reading body language."

Truth.

Although, whether or not it was a truth she could trust, she didn't know. Everything about Trick screamed a lie, even though his words had always appeared to be honest.

"So, why are you sad?"

"I am a blood slave."

"Nope, not buying it. You chose this."

She sighed. It was unfortunate that he was intelligent. "I was reminiscing about Heaven."

He flicked her a sharp glance. "Which bit?"

"I was thinking about how the archangel Gabriel would have loved a tool like this. I used to be in service to him."

"I thought you were one of the guards for Heaven's Heart."

Surprise flooded her, followed by wry amusement. Of course he would know that. Trick seemed to know all the important gossip. *Except how to interpret emojis.* That little oversight made him more appealing, however.

"I guarded the Heart for the past fifty years. Before that I was a scout."

"You must have been fast."

"One of the very fastest."

An emotion almost like pity darkened the warm brown of his eyes. Resentment welled within her in response.

"I do not mourn my wings." And that was true. To grieve their loss acknowledged that she may never fly again. "I will earn them back."

"Ahhh. They gave you an impossible task and somehow you will achieve it."

"Nothing is impossible." She could not believe otherwise.

He gave her a sad smile. "Darling, if only that were true. The legends about fallen angels state that they are always given a way back into Heaven, but not one has ever achieved it. Even Lucifer was given a get-out-of-jail-free card."

"What was his task?" In Heaven, everyone focused on Lucifer's fall—*not* his potential return.

Trick spun the model of the Hell-lord's abode until it

became a glimmering blur. "Give up the mantle of Hell-lord, beg for mercy on his knees, and save the soul of an impure."

"What is an 'impure'?" Perhaps that was something she could also ask Raze.

"That was never defined."

"But the other conditions are obtainable. And he could learn the meaning of impure."

"If you've ever met Lucifer, you'll know that he would never relinquish power. It is not in his nature." He stopped the spinning plan with a finger. "Lucifer would rather die than beg for anything."

"How do you know that?"

Trick gave a negligent shrug. "I asked him."

CHAPTER 18

Naturally, she is awe-inspiring even when she is shocked.

Surely there had been sonnets written to her beauty.

The worst part, though? Seraphina looked perfect in his rooms. And the glittering golden light between them didn't help—it only served to highlight her physical perfection.

"You asked *Lucifer* about it?" Disbelief had widened her eyes and softened her mouth.

The urge to kiss her again sizzled through him, hard to resist.

But then annoyance washed through him. *Now is not the time to make out with her. In fact, it will never be the right time again.* He should never have done it. It would have been better to never know her taste, to never know the feel of her against him...

Seraphina poked him with one long, elegant finger, making him jolt. "Are you listening to me?"

"No." He shook himself. *Idiot.* "But I am now."

Stop mooning over her. You're worse with her than you were with Dru. And he'd known Dru decades.

But you never kissed Dru.

"You actually asked Lucifer about the conditions of his re-ascension?"

"I did."

"And he let you?"

"He did."

"But...why?"

"I met with every Hell-lord when it came to set up my guild." *Truth.* He couldn't lie or she'd know... "And I asked them each a series of questions I thought was relevant to the guild's interests. And to my well-being."

"And you decided on Hades, not Lucifer, after that interrogation?"

"Just because Lucifer was once an angel, it doesn't make him better suited to being my overlord. Hades fit the bill."

Lucifer had come across as a smarmy jerk, Satan as psychotic, and Hades as ruthless but practical. It was the latter that had won Trick over. Lucifer wouldn't put anything above his own self-interest, even his own damned pride, and Satan was rumored to have a thing for his half-sister, which was all kinds of disgusting, even for a demon. Hades stuck to his deals and Trick needed someone who wouldn't turn on him the moment the tide changed.

Which is why this whole seven-day-or-your-dead-thing is really out of character. The contract still hadn't come through, either. Normally, Trick would refuse to work without the paperwork in place, but this was Hades. You did as he asked, or else bad things happened to you.

Seraphina looked...confused, for want of a better

word.

"What is it?" Trick asked.

"You think Lucifer isn't good enough to work for?"

"He's the first fallen angel. He got kicked out of Heaven by God, not by the other archangels. And anyway, just because someone is an angel, it doesn't make them intrinsically a good person. Angels still do bad things."

Her gaze turned fierce for a moment, as if she would argue, but then she shook her head. "You're right."

This conversation was getting a bit too heavy. "I always am."

She snorted in derision, but at least he'd lightened the mood.

Her phone chimed, and she fished it out of a tight back pocket. A smile broke over her face, the expression radiant with triumph. "I have something."

"Your phone, yes."

She rolled her eyes. "My contact at the Cat on a Broomstick came through."

"You mean *the* Theodora Broome actually agreed to work with you?"

Trick had been trying to get spells from the Crone for decades, but she'd told him no deal. Wouldn't even agree to meet with him in person to hear his case.

Seraphina smirked. "More than once."

"Fine." Trick spun the crystal on the coffee table three times to turn off the display, then pocketed it. "Let's go."

"Go where?"

"To get the intel."

"I will go alone."

"You can waste another Devilsgate spell, or I could

just teleport you to the shop. Either way, I'll follow you."

She scowled. "Fine."

Trick came around the coffee table and held out his hand.

"What's that for?"

"So I can teleport you."

"Can't you do it without?"

"It would use up a lot of power, unnecessarily. It's easier to have an anchor."

"What do you mean?"

"When you're with the person you want to teleport, touching them serves as an anchor. Seeing them does it, but takes more power. If they were somewhere else—and I wanted to teleport to them—they'd need to have something familiar on them. Something to lock onto, hence the anchor."

"I see."

Sighing, she placed her palm in his, the contact searing in its intensity. *Maybe you should sleep with her, just so this attraction will go away.* It was a crazy idea, but one he'd have to think about some more. He concentrated, and then they were in a side alley near the Cat on a Broomstick. Rather silly name for the shop, but Trick wasn't about to let Theodora know he thought that.

Seraphina dropped his hand like it was a bomb about to go off, then strode around the corner and toward the store. She paused at the threshold, waiting for him to catch up.

"We just storm inside?" he asked.

"We go inside like regular people." With that, she opened the door and stepped into an asthmatic's worst nightmare.

Trick winced at the pungent hit of incense, while avidly taking in the contents of the shop. He'd been here once before, some fifty years ago. His time inside had been *very* short-lived after being kicked out by a blue-haired termagant who'd been the owner at the time.

Theodora's mother, if he was correct in his recollection.

Half-expecting her to leap out at him any second now, he followed Seraphina in a winding course around sets of drawers, tables and glass display cases. They reached the counter, where a brown-haired youth sat playing on his iPhone.

Seraphina cleared her throat.

"Welcome to Cat on a Broomstick. How can I help you?" He didn't even bother looking up from his device.

Suddenly, a hand came out of the shadows behind the counter and thwacked the teenager on the back of the head, making him fumble his phone. "Ow!" But he didn't rub his head as he was too busy juggling the cell he'd nearly dropped. He turned back to his assailant. "Gran!"

"I told you no phones at the counter."

"But I was just checking a message..."

"You didn't even look up."

"Whatever." But he spun around on his chair to face them, stopping with a lurch the moment he spotted Seraphina.

There it is.

The dumbstruck look of awe that humans must feel when faced by the fallen angel.

I hope I kept my mouth shut.

The old lady—Gran—emerged into the light, and tapped the boy hard on the shoulder. Power flew from her in a steady stream. This same little old lady had delivered Seraphina's lipstick to the guild *and* hit on him in the process. But the elderly woman wasn't looking at Trick, this time. Instead, she growled at her grandson. "Shut your mouth, you're embarrassing yourself."

Obediently, the boy closed his jaw.

"I'll be out the back. If you play with your phone again in front of a customer, I will burn it."

"Gran!"

"I wonder how fast it will take to catch fire?" the witch said, stalking toward a door ten feet away.

Seraphina and Trick followed.

Is this Theodora Broome?

The aura of power—something she'd muted when visiting the Halcyon Guild back in Tartarus—was too strong for her to be anything other than a Crone. *I always wanted a witch as part of the guild.*

Maybe he could talk to Theodora about arranging a placement? He didn't even have to enslave them.

The Crone stood at the door, then waved a hand at them. "In."

Seraphina swept inside, Trick close on her heels. She sat on a small sofa, and while normally he'd take the seat next to her, just to unsettle her, he decided on pulling out a chair from the small table. He didn't particularly want to unsettle himself.

"So, you said you had something?" Seraphina said into the quiet.

"Thanks for the introduction," the Crone muttered, then batted her eyelashes at Trick.

"How rude of me." But Seraphina looked more amused than chastised. "This is Trick, ruler of the

Halcyon Guild. Trick, this is Theodora Broome, Crone of the witches."

He smiled, flashing his pearly whites. "It is such a pleasure to finally meet you. You didn't have a time to introduce yourself last time."

She humphed, then sat down next to Seraphina. "Call me Dora. Can you take off your shirt?"

He narrowed his eyes. "Why do I need to do that?"

"Research." Dora leered at him.

"She's hitting on me again," Trick said. He was almost flattered.

Seraphina shook her head. "We're wasting time. Back to business. You said Rowan found something in her search."

Dora shot him an apologetic look, like Seraphina was ruining all their fun.

"I'll let her tell you." Dora whipped out her own cell. "Pfft. Dorian out there has the newest model of iPhone. I should make him swap it with mine, for being such a pain in the ass."

"Who is Rowan?" Trick asked. Seraphina had yet to fill him in on the details.

"She's my granddaughter and she doesn't believe in magic. So, keep any talk of it to yourself, got it?"

That only led to more questions, but he nodded. Perhaps if he made a good impression on Dora, she'd work with him in the future.

The door opened and a redheaded woman burst inside, a book clutched in her hands. "I found it! I found the replica."

CHAPTER 19

Trick mouthed the word 'Replica?' at Seraphina, but she ignored his query. She'd explain it all later.

"So where is the spear? The replica?" Seraphina had moved half out of her seat as she asked the question. Catching Dora's look, which Yael would translate as 'calm your farm', she lowered herself back into place.

You can't go marching off just yet.

Dina's voice in her mind.

Dina? she called out telepathically.

But there was no answer.

It's just your imagination; your thoughts sounding like her voice. If Dina was really speaking to her, it wouldn't be for some small warning. Surely she would say where she was being kept, how she fared? How they could find her...

"It's here!" Rowan opened the book that had been clutched to her chest and thrust it out at them. Her fingers covered half a photo, but Seraphina read the caption beneath.

"*Purported replica of the* Amenonuhoko," Trick

murmured. "Do you really think this is it?"

"Wait." Rowan pulled the book back to her chest, then eyed Trick like he was diseased. Seraphina could sympathize with the thought, but was surprised the woman had reacted in such a way. Trick was nothing if not pretty to look at.

"Who is he?" Rowan asked.

"This is my business associate, Mr. Trick," Seraphina said.

"Trick?" An auburn eyebrow rose skeptically.

"What? Your surname is Broome."

Dora skewered him with a dagger-sharp look.

"I said I'd give this information to you, not to every man and his dog," Rowan said.

"I am only one person, and I don't own any dogs," Trick commented.

The guild had a strict no-pets rule—Seraphina had seen that in the welcome pack. He gave the girl a charming smile, and Seraphina was surprised that it only seemed to strengthen her resolve *against* him.

I think I like her.

Rowan was moral, upright, and had an instinctive wariness about Trick. All of which impressed Seraphina.

"Rowan, please. They are business partners working together." Dora's voice was stern, yet also slightly pleading.

"Fine." Rowan tossed the book at Seraphina.

She caught it in one hand, then flipped it over so she could read the cover. "*A Catalogue of the Private Collection of Luke M. Starre?*"

Trick hovered near her elbow. He smelled spicy, like an expensive cologne. "Morning Star."

Luke was short for Lucifer, she realized. And Lucifer translated to 'bearer of light' or the 'morning star'...

"He doesn't believe in being inconspicuous, does he?" Seraphina whispered.

"I told you, the guy has no style."

She wasn't about to quibble over that. Louder, she said, "It says this is a catalogue of a private collection?"

"Yes." Rowan nodded, tucking a strand of fiery hair behind her ear as she did so. "This guy has an immense one. Half of the items have a provenance listed, but a lot don't. Your spear is one of the ones that doesn't. Which makes sense, in a way, if it's a replica." Rowan paced the small area. "But it also says it was created in the sixth century CE, which means that it would have been made soon after Shinto was described in literary records."

Seraphina could feel Trick's curiosity burning like a torch, but she ignored it. "Thank you for this."

Rowan turned to them. "This artifact was probably stolen. But if you get it back, how will you know which family to give it to?"

"We can't reveal the identity of our client. But it will be returned to the proper hands." The words left a bitter taste in her mouth.

"I really do hope you give it back to the Japanese people. It's theirs, not this Luke's, or anyone else's. Uh, where are you going with that?" Rowan held out a hand for the book.

"Home, to read it." The more knowledge she had about this spear and its location, the better.

Rowan frowned.

She wanted to tell the girl, *I do sympathize with your beliefs, but when a god wants something, he gets it.* But the girl wouldn't believe her, and Seraphina's warrior training had not really prepared her for this. *Gods are meant to smite you, not humor you.*

"It's a library book, I can't let you do that. It's in my name."

"Could we at least borrow it so we can scan the relevant pages?" Trick asked.

"I guess..."

"I have an app on my phone. I can do it right now." Trick took the book from Seraphina, his fingers brushing hers, sending sparks along her nerve endings.

She nearly winced.

I don't like that my body is so aware of his.

Trick flipped the book closed, and held his phone over it, taking a picture. He then worked his way through the tome, with Rowan pointing him to the relevant pages. She seemed relieved at this solution.

I could have paid the fine or replaced the book.

But in a way, she understood. She wouldn't have wanted to lend her weapons out to anyone she did not trust, and books, Seraphina realized, were Rowan's weapons—or her defense.

"Done!" Trick handed the redhead the book.

"Thanks."

Dora stood, leaning over slightly with the effort. "I will email you the bill."

Seraphina flashed the witch a smile and nodded at Trick. "Don't email me, email *him*."

The guild owner rolled his eyes. "Lucky me."

"Holy fucking cow. Did you even bother to negotiate the rate?" Trick asked, staring at his phone.

Seraphina glanced at him. "Do you have to cuss so much?"

He looked at her like she was crazy. "I live in Hell, I run an assassination guild. Of course, I do."

They were back in his quarters, the golden-flecked crystal dormant on the table between them. Papers were spread either side of the gem; copies of the book Rowan had found, plans of Lucifer's residences, and the addresses of each.

"It can't be that costly. Dora charges a fair rate," Seraphina replied. She returned her attention to the pages from the artifact book. He'd taken more photographs than she'd realized.

"Thirty grand just for telling us about a book. The guild gets paid less than that for some assassinations."

"I wouldn't get out of bed for less than one hundred thousand dollars," Seraphina replied, picking up another the page. Although, saying that, Azrael had done most of the wet work. But not all. "You need to up your rates."

"I have to be competitive. I can't just pick and choose what I want—I have forty people here who need work."

So they can buy their freedom.

Was it wrong of her to admire the fact he wanted to enable them to do so?

"Just pass the bill on to Hades."

"Invoice him for it?" Trick rubbed his chin. "But he's a god."

"Who employed you to do a job. If this was the Falling Star, I'd be invoicing him for all expenses, unless I offered a flat fee. Since he gave you the job, charge him whatever it costs. His fault for not negotiating, and for threatening us with death if we fail."

"Good point."

She ran her fingers over the copied pages of the book. *Rowan is right*, she thought, *Lucifer does have an immense collection of artifacts*. Perhaps even greater than the one possessed by Set, the former Egyptian god of chaos. Azrael and Dru had raided his fortress a few weeks ago to steal Odin's Orb. It hadn't been an easy mission; they'd been attacked by a dragon, trapped in a Devilsnare, and had to behead the god to escape.

Although, that wasn't enough to kill Set, apparently.

Revenge would no doubt follow them.

I will be there to help when it does.

Assuming she could survive the next few days and pay off her debt.

Once they entered Lucifer's stronghold, they would have to avoid any and all conflict with the fallen angel. They couldn't risk engaging him in a battle. *He will be stronger than Trick and I combined.* And they had up to seven such strongholds to investigate.

Trick spun the crystal in its pattern, and the plan of a large mansion appeared. "Despite the size of this place, it can't possibly house all of Lucifer's artifacts. Only the Tower of Tortures can, and Baal—I mean, Laird—didn't think it was there."

"His information is out of date, but we can ask around."

"I already have Sylvester on it." Trick rotated the mansion.

"This book was published ten years ago. Do you think that the catalogue's contents might still be in the Human

Realm? He would have had to have brought his collection there for inventory."

"Only if the person doing the recording was human."

"Hrm." She flipped back to the page outlining the author's details, but 'Charity Smythe-Wilson' didn't give much away.

"How many demons would call their children Charity?"

"I'd like to say none, but some might do it out of spite." Trick shrugged. "Or it's a pseudonym."

Reaching for the list provided by Sylvester and Laird, Seraphina read, "Lucifer has three residences in the Human Realm."

"Then we will have to search all three."

CHAPTER 20

Trick shoved a handful of spells into a backpack, moved his garrote to a better position, added a few throwing stars, and then slid a slim electronic tablet into its designated pocket. They had three houses to search, to start with, and four days left to do it. The first one was in Miami, the second in Iceland, and the third, New Zealand, near Hobbiton.

Go figure.

He'd never taken Lucifer for a Tolkien fan, but who knew?

"The book says that the collection was reviewed in his Miami residence," Seraphina said. She was dressed head to toe in black tactical gear and bristled with weapons. She was already wearing a small backpack chock-full of spells.

"Yes, which makes me think it won't be there anymore." He doubted Lucifer would have kept the entire collection in one place—especially if humans had catalogued it.

"But you think Iceland is the next likely option?" Her

voice betrayed her skepticism.

"His residence is near Dimmuborgir."

"I am unfamiliar with this place, is it dangerous?"

Trick stared at her. "You're an angel and you don't know? In Icelandic tradition, it is said to be the place where Satan landed after he fell from Heaven. But we all know Satan has never stepped foot in Heaven—so it's referring to Lucifer and his fall."

"It is but one human tradition."

"In this case, they're right." Lucifer was the first angel to be cast from Heaven—his wings gone, his pride bloated, and his power immense. He'd crash-landed in a volcano and had lived. Dimmuborgir had formed as a result. Human scientists had dated the lava flow to only be a little over two thousand years old, but the original formation was much older than that.

"If he chose Iceland because of its relevance to his fall, why Miami and New Zealand?" Seraphina asked.

"I've no idea. Maybe the summer climate of Miami reminds him of Hell? As for the New Zealand location, maybe he liked the *Lord of the Rings*?" That trilogy he *had* read. Sylvester had tried to force him to watch the movies, but they were way lengthy, and he struggled to sit still for more than an hour at a time. Trick had to stay busy. Forget that. As the ruler of a mercenary guild, he *was* busy.

Besides, when you actually knew how to fight with a sword, watching actors do it was almost painful.

"Who is this Lord of the Rings?" Seraphina asked, putting her hands on her hips. The fallen angel appeared ready to tackle this new menace bare-handed if need be.

I'd love to see her do it.

"Tolkien."

"I've never heard of him. Is he a powerful sorcerer?"

"He was actually a linguist."

"Really. Huh." Seraphina looked impressed.

He didn't have the heart to tell her it was all fictional. *Maybe later, when she isn't wearing quite so many weapons.*

How about when she isn't wearing anything at all?

Gritting his teeth, he chose to ignore that thought and accompanying blood rush to his groin. He wasn't a teenager anymore—hadn't been for millennia. He should be able to control his baser urges.

But why would you want to?

Normally, he'd have agreed with that idea wholeheartedly, but it was foolish to do so this time. *Angels are not to be messed with. This one would rather slit my throat than fuck me.*

The reminder only served to enflame his libido more.

He sighed.

Why do I have a thing for powerful women?

"How are we going to get into Lucifer's residence?" Seraphina demanded.

"That's where Sylvester comes in. He'll get us in, but we only have an hour or two to look around. We'll have to be fast."

"This place is a labyrinth." She indicated the still-glowing 3D image. "Two hours won't be long enough."

He tied a GoPro to the shoulder strap on his backpack. He should put it on his head, but he hated the feel of the band. "It's all we have. We'll have to be quick."

"It's cold," Seraphina murmured shortly after Trick teleported them to Dimmuborgir. Snow dusted almost every surface, with a few hints of greenery visible against the stark whiteness. Large protruding crags of solidified lava were visible across the snowscape, and the taste of ancient magic was thick in the air.

They were in the right location.

"Put your hood on." Trick glanced at her as she rubbed her cheeks with gloved hands. "I thought angels weren't meant to feel the cold."

Grumbling, she tucked her face inside the fur-lined hood. "I've never liked the cold."

"It's chilly when you're flying at altitude."

She shot him a sharp glance, then focused on the bleak landscape before them. "I learned how to block the pain out. But I still don't like it."

Sylvester appeared next to them. He was dressed in a black turtleneck sweater and black cargo pants, the pockets filled to the brim with goodies. The cambion gave a low whistle as the dying sun bled red and pink across the sky. "I don't see any house. You said there'd be a house."

"It's cloaked by magic," Trick said. "I can feel it."

"This should help then." The cambion tugged a locket from under his shirt.

"Is that a Clear Sight spell?" Trick asked, staring at the engraving of a wide-open eye on the face of the locket.

"Sure is." Then he muttered, "At least you get it. Dru gave me shit for it when she saw it."

Trick barely felt a pang of regret at the mention of Dru. *How fickle you are.*

Maybe he really did have a thing for unobtainable

women. Seraphina was about as unobtainable as you could get.

Sylvester opened the clasp of the locket, revealing what looked like dark eyeshadow inside. The cambion delicately ran a finger through the powder, then rubbed it on each eyelid. It was a smoky color—all it served to do was make Sylvester's baby-blue eyes even bluer.

"We're putting on makeup?" Seraphina asked, dubious. But she reached over anyway, dabbed a finger in the magical eyeshadow, and applied it as Sylvester had.

Trick did the same. His eyelids stung for a moment, making him blink rapidly. Once the irritation had faded, though, his eyesight was better than it had ever been.

And a great hulking monolith of a house had appeared, perched between stony outcrops.

It was barely three hundred yards away. Thousands of tourists would travel past it each year without being any wiser as to its existence.

It is rather brilliant.

He didn't like giving Lucifer any credit, but this was some powerful magic at play. He noticed some of the glyphs and symbols used in the spell work—apparent now he wore the eyeshadow—were not angelic in origin.

He'd hired sorcerers.

And from the hieroglyphics involved, Set was one of them.

So why had Set lived in Satan's realm—Inferno—and not in Sheol with Lucifer?

Something to be pondered at a later date.

"Impressive," Sylvester said, eyeing the architecture.

Seraphina snorted. "It's ostentatious."

"Ostentatious? I would have said it was a Brutalist nightmare." It was large, blocky, and had huge soaring windows punctuated by concrete pillars.

"This would have been built before Brutalism was even a thing," Sylvester said.

"Maybe it was the inspiration?"

"Yeah, except nobody can see it."

"But people can see *us*." Seraphina snapped.

"Do your thing." Trick waved a hand at her.

"Do what thing?"

"Angels can make themselves and others invisible with a blood spell. Get cracking."

Surprise gave her pause, then she nodded, and grabbed a knife. She ran it down her forearm and watched the blood seep for a moment. It was dark red against the ebony of her skin. "Come here."

Both Sylvester and Trick stepped forward. With her blood, she drew a glyph in ancient angelic on both of their chests, before doing the same to herself. Nothing happened.

"I can still see us all," Sylvester muttered.

"That is because we're wearing the Clear Sight spell." Trick rolled his eyes.

"Oh yeah."

Checking the time, Seraphina asked, "Okay, is everyone ready?"

"Yep." Sylvester nodded.

"We have two hours before the invisibility spell will fade."

"Let's go."

Chapter 21

Seraphina stood to the side as Trick and Sylvester worked the locks on the rear door of Lucifer's Icelandic mansion. The two demons worked efficiently, like they had done this a hundred times before. The door was glass and aluminum, but it blazed with numerous spells, many written in angelic, many in other strange texts. *I should have brought Raze.* The locks themselves were almost blinding in their intensity.

"Done." Sylvester backed away from the door and wiped his gloved hands on his pants. "I'm out of here. I can't be caught near Lucifer's place, or he will tie it back to Laird."

Seraphina put her phone away in a pocket. She'd had it to hand in case she needed to call Raze for a translation, but Sylvester hadn't needed any help.

"Even you call him that?" Trick asked, putting a pair of sunglasses away in his backpack.

"It's his preferred one," Sylvester replied, leaving his Aviators on.

"He should just use his real one."

Sylvester raised an auburn eyebrow. "So should you."

"Who says Trick isn't my real name?"

"What's your first name, then?"

"It's a mononym. You know, like Cher, Prince, Pink."

"*Pink*?"

"What? I like her music. She's got a sense of humor."

This was wasting time.

"I have no idea who you are talking about," Seraphina hissed, "but can you save the banter for later, when we're done?"

"Sure thing, angel lady." Sylvester saluted her, then vanished.

She spun to face Trick. "He can teleport?"

"Clearly."

She ground her teeth. She thought he'd used a spell when he'd arrived in Iceland, but the thief could come and go as he pleased. *It would be nice to know the full potential of my colleagues, so I know how to use them to their best advantage.*

She'd talk to Trick about getting proper run-downs on her fellow guild members. For now, she had a house to infiltrate.

"We do this just like we planned. Together, and fast." Trick stared, as if daring her to argue.

She glanced around, but they were still alone. And there wasn't a security camera in sight. Was Lucifer that confident?

"I still think splitting up would be better."

"Can you teleport?"

"No."

"Then we stick together."

Rolling her eyes behind his back, she fell into place.

"I saw that," he muttered.

They entered Lucifer's house.

In the mud room, they dried their boots off, and stashed the towels in their packs. The floors were made of a shiny pale timber, and the walls a brilliant white. Quickly, they made their way through the entrance, then up a staircase. According to the plan she'd memorized, the lower levels of the house were reserved for garaging, the kitchen, a sauna, and a laundry room. The upper floors housed the living areas, formal meeting areas, and bedrooms.

It was all very...plain, really.

It wasn't until they hurried into a long gallery that things got interesting. Paintings lined one wall, while the other was a sheet of floor-to-ceiling glass that saturated the area with sunlight. Glass and chrome cabinets lined the center of the room, each housing an artifact. More spells glowed on the display cases, and near the paintings.

"It's like it's a museum," she said quietly.

"He doesn't live here, so it probably is treated as one. A memorial—or testament—to his fall from grace."

"Be careful. This place has modern security, as well as magic."

"But no cameras."

"None we can see. But we're invisible, so it doesn't matter."

They split up, one walking each side of the cabinets. Wonder filled her at the rare pieces within. *The Veil of Isis. Járngreipr. The Ring of Dispel.* The magical items covered a cross-section of religions, legends, and beliefs. But there was no spear.

She reached the end of the gallery, disappointment weighing heavy in her stomach. "It's not here."

"There's another gallery on this floor."

They turned right at the end of the long room and moved silently toward the second gallery. This, too, was bright and airy, but because the ceiling was crafted from glass, rather than the walls. Both sides of the space had long display cases, the natural light illuminating the treasures within.

"I'll take the left one," Trick said.

She hurried to the right-hand side of the hall, her eyes sweeping the artifacts and their labels with quick precision. *Fragment of Draconite, Marseille, France, 7th Century BCE*. Then a large pendant, housing nine different gemstones, labelled *Navaratna, 18th Century CE*. The next item was a piece of metal, shaped like a lightning bolt. The sign read: *One of the hundred bolts sent by Zeus, the Greek God, when he killed Typhon. Zeus was killed in stage two of the Great Culling. 2nd Century CE.*

There were so many wonders here.

I can see why Rowan Broome thinks a museum should house them.

But the humans would never believe these were real—they would call them replicas or fakes, with no material worth. Their lack of provenance was due to their magical nature; when objects were created through powerful sorcery, or battles that had taken place in the skies, under the earth, in the sea...there were no names for such locations.

She reached the end of the gallery, with no sign of the spear.

Frustration welled within her. They were already at

day three. They had but four more days to find and retrieve this spear.

Trick joined her. "No luck for me."

"None for me, either."

"Let's try the next floor." Trick turned to go back the way he came.

The third gallery had a glass ceiling as well as transparent walls. It was so bright, she squinted against the illumination, her eyesight barely able to register the glow from the protection spells. There were only seven cabinets here, and each housed only a single item.

"This seems more likely."

Excitement urged her to hurry, but they had to be careful. Even though they were invisible, she couldn't risk setting off any spells accidentally. The last thing they needed was Lucifer's attention.

"How much longer until our invisibility spell wears off?" Trick asked.

She checked her watch. "Forty minutes."

"Plenty of time."

Green light glimmered at the edge of her vision, but this hall was so bright, it was difficult to see if there was a spell near the cabinet or not. As Trick walked toward the first display case, his shadow cast over the shiny wooden floor. She lunged toward the demon, trying to pull him back, but it was too late.

As her hand met his backpack, Trick vanished, and a millisecond later, so did she.

Seraphina hit the ground hard, the wind momentarily

knocked out of her. She lay on her back, trying to convince her lungs it was okay to breathe. When she next opened her eyes, there was nothing but inky darkness. Panic gripped her, until she realized her lack of vision was because they were someplace dark, not because the spell had sent her blind. Her eyesight soon adjusted to the gloom.

Rough stone walls soared around and above them, while iron bars punched from the floor to the roof, trapping them inside.

Her stomach sank. They were in a cell. The scent of sulfur was thick in the air, the rotten-egg odor nauseating. It wasn't this strong in the guild.

"This isn't good," Trick mumbled. He was lying on his side, arm cradled to his chest.

"Are you hurt?" She sat up, reaching a hand out to him.

He pulled himself up with a grunt, ignoring her proffered help. "Broken arm. It will heal soon."

"We're in a cell."

"No, we're underground, back in Hell. It's a dungeon. Probably in the Tower of Tortures."

"Can you be sure?" Her eyes swept over him, but aside from dirt smudged on his cheek and his injured arm, he appeared well enough. Still handsome as sin.

"No."

"Then we might be able to escape."

"Sure, and Uriel might come down here, kiss our feet, and give you your wings back."

"What do you mean by that?"

He leaned his head against the wall behind him, exposing the long stretch of his throat. "I mean we're screwed."

CHAPTER 22

Trick's arm hurt like…well, Hell.

But it would mend. Broken bones always did. And courtesy of his ties to the guild and the power they granted, it would only take a few hours, rather than the two days it would have normally taken someone like him. *The guild.* Great. With no one to manage them, they'd probably descend into chaos by the end of the week. Managing so many diverse demon species required a firm hand and delicate balance. Without him around to control things...

Don't worry about it yet. You'll get out.

Sure, and the sky is pink in the Human Realm.

First things first.

Trick tried to teleport, but nothing happened. *Damnit.* The cell had spells to counteract teleportation. *Lucifer would be foolish to have otherwise.* Trick had the same magical wards on his own cells.

"Surely we can escape from here." Seraphina stood and walked to the cell's bars, gripping them with her hands. He opened his mouth to issue a warning, but too late. She hissed and sprung back, staring at her palms as if they had betrayed her. "That *hurt*."

"There's magic on the bars."

She frowned, rubbing her palms against her shirt. "I couldn't see it."

"The Clear Sight spell must have worn off." It was almost gone for him, too. He could just see the faintest shimmers of magic. *If that damned gallery hadn't been so bright, I would have seen the trap before we walked into it.* But the combination of his fading spell and the room's brilliance had been a deadly combination.

You got cocky.

What was done was done.

You should have known better. Arrogance gets you nowhere.

Like humility was any better.

"We don't even know if the spear was in there," Seraphina moaned the last half of the sentence. She took the three steps back to him, and slumped down against the wall, her hands held out as if burned.

Metal grated against stone, and the clomp of heavy footsteps approached. Trick held a hand up to his lips. If they were still invisible, then the guard might report no one had been teleported in...

It might give them a small window to escape and a small chance was better than no chance.

An armored Elock demon appeared, his massive horns protruding from a metal helmet, and fur wavering on his flat nose. He looked around the cell with beady eyes, before scratching his head and shrugging.

Trick held his breath until the demon turned away, lumbering back in the direction he'd come. He didn't turn back to Seraphina until the sound of grinding metal reached them.

"I think we've just bought ourselves a couple of hours." He thought of her disappointment and said, "Maybe we can find out if the spear was in the final gallery." With one hand, he unstrapped the GoPro, and then swung his pack around. He quickly hooked the camera up to his tablet, and replayed the last few minutes of footage.

"You filmed it?" She scooted closer, her warmth like a brand against his side.

"Yep, just in case we needed to have another look at anything." He zoomed in on the glass cases. While the labels weren't legible, the artifacts *were*. "Sword, shield, dress, gemstones, basket, tea towel, and a bit of wool. Nothing that looks like a spear."

"Let me have a look."

He handed the fallen angel the tablet. She scanned the images with a frown of concentration. "You're right. There's nothing that looks like a spear." She zoomed in on the wool fragment.

"What, you don't believe my analysis?" He held a hand up to his heart. "I'm wounded."

It's better she doesn't trust you. She's less likely to sleep with you that way.

She never was going to anyway.

Great, now I am talking to myself.

Instead of arguing with his own mind, he should be focusing on a way out. But the thing was, no one had ever escaped Lucifer's Tower of Tortures before. There was a reason it had the name it did, poor use of alliteration notwithstanding.

Pulling out his cellphone, he narrowed his eyes in surprise. He had one tiny bar of reception. Not enough to call out on...but maybe he could send an SOS to Hades?

Seraphina looked up from the tablet. "What are you doing?"

"I have reception."

"You *do*?"

"I'll message Hades."

"No, message Raze, he'll get us out."

The hulking black-skinned angel with cloud-colored eyes? He thought not.

"Your fallen angel buddy will get us out? Of the Tower of Tortures?" Trick's voice dripped with disbelief.

"Fine. Message Hades." Seraphina folded her arms, the tablet resting in her lap.

"That's what I was planning on doing."

And he had to do it before his battery died. It was losing a percent a second, almost. *Must take extra power to hold the signal here.*

STUCK IN TOWER OF TORTURES' DUNGEON. PLEASE BREAK US OUT. LUCIFER MAY NOT REALIZE WE'RE HERE.

Succinct and to the point. He hit send.

A few seconds later, his phone beeped.

I CAN'T BREAK YOU OUT. YOU KNOW THAT. (AND HOW'D YOU GET TRAPPED AND LUCIFER NOT KNOW?)

Disappointment arched through him.

"What? What did he say?" Seraphina tried to snatch the phone out of his hand.

He yanked it away. "You have a nasty habit of grabbing shit that isn't yours."

"Sorry," she said, then under her breath added, "so not sorry."

"You've been spending too much time with Dru," he growled. That was the sort of thing she'd say.

"*Well?*"

"He says he can't get us out."

"I *said* we should have messaged Raze."

"Hush."

He typed again.

FIND SOMEONE WHO CAN GET US OUT. WE ARE CURRENTLY INVISIBLE.

WHY DID YOU GET CAUGHT?

ACCIDENT WHILE LOOKING FOR THE HJS.

He got an eye-rolling emoji in response.

Fucker.

He sent an emoji back—despite his dislike of the things—with a finger flipping the bird.

I'LL DO WHAT I CAN.

WE ONLY HAVE FOUR MORE DAYS.

STUPID OF YOU TO GET CAUGHT. G2G, NEED TO SPANK SOME SOULS.

Trick didn't know if that was literal or figurative, and he decided not to ask. His phone was down to twenty percent battery power anyway.

He relayed the messages to Seraphina, then asked, "Should I turn it off to conserve power?"

"I think I have a portable charger in my pack." But she made no move to get it.

"I'll turn it off."

"But we might lose reception."

"Either way, we won't have it for long."

She nodded, tiredness suddenly apparent on her face.

For good measure, he took a selfie of himself and Seraphina and sent it to Hades before shutting down the phone and rummaging through his pack for medical supplies. "When did you last sleep?"

"Three days ago."

"Have a rest now."

"No."

"Fine. Show me your hands."

He expected her to argue and was surprised when she held out her palms. The skin was reddened, but there were no blisters.

"Here, rub some of this on it." He handed her a small packet of cream, careful not to make contact.

She did as instructed, before passing it back. "Thanks."

He stowed everything away, but for the tablet, which remained in her lap. He shifted against the wall, trying to ease the discomfort in his arm while it healed. "What were you looking at? On the video."

"The piece of wool. It looked gold. I wondered if it wasn't wool, but one of Lucifer's old feathers."

"That alone would be worth a fortune. But it could be a piece of the golden fleece."

"From Greek legend?"

"Yup."

"For a demon, you sure know a lot about mythology and angels." Seraphina passed him the tablet, careful not to smear cream on the screen.

"I told you, information is my thing. The more I know, the better off I am."

It wasn't just done for profit, although that was a motivating factor. Originally, he'd had to do it for survival. Hell was a harsh place, and he needed to know who he was working with, for, or against. One misstep and it would have been all over for him.

Now...*now* it was a slight addiction.

He liked having the scoop on his enemies, friends and lovers. It gave him a kick to work out people's secret identities, like he had Baal's. *Knowledge is power.* And Trick intended never to be weak again. He honed his mind like he did his body—until it was a weapon he could use to win any and every fight.

Seraphina tilted her chin down, so she was looking at the ground. "What did Uriel want?"

She must have been dying to ask that for days.

"To buy Z back."

Her shoulders tensed. "Would you have sold him?"

That answer was easy. "Nope."

"Why not?"

"Because Uriel is an asshole."

She made a half-laughing, half-choking sound. "He is an *archangel*."

"Doesn't stop him from being an asshole. He offered to hand over an unfallen angel to take Z's place."

"*What?*" Her head turned to face him so quickly he thought she might get whiplash.

"He would have sacrificed some poor angel to get Z back. Why, though? To just banish him again?"

Seraphina stared at the ground. "They might have forgiven Z."

Trick scowled. "You can't believe that. They took *your* wings, and you weren't even on duty at the time."

"How do you know that?"

"I know how the Heart is guarded—two angels at all

times. If Z was kidnapped, then the other angel on duty was probably also taken, and since you weren't sold to me as a slave..." he let the sentence trail off.

"How do you know there are only two guards at any one time?"

"We've been over my love for information."

She sighed. "Can that love break us out?"

CHAPTER 23

The cream Trick had given her had helped with the ache in Seraphina's palms, but she could fight if needed to. She'd been trained to engage in combat while suffering all kinds of pain and injuries. Her masters had broken limbs, simply so she could be taught to hold a sword through the agony. Mildly burned hands were nothing.

She checked her watch. Just past midnight. Only three days left.

Standing, she walked the three steps to the doorway, and peered out, careful to keep the skin of her face away from the bars. More cells were spaced evenly along a corridor that blended into shadow at either end. There were no signs, and it didn't look like there were any other prisoners. She couldn't even see the door the flat-nosed demon had used to enter their cellblock.

"You sure we're in the Tower of Tortures?" she asked over her shoulder.

"We aren't in the Human Realm. They wouldn't station an Elock demon out there, even with Lucifer's approval. They have a penchant for human flesh—a lot of it. We must be in one of his four Hell residences. It makes sense we are in the Tower."

She sat again, leaning her head against the cool stone wall. "If Hades doesn't come through, then we're stuck here. The invisibility spell will wear off in about ten minutes, and the next time the guard comes, we'll be seen."

"Did you pack any spells that can cut through warded doors?" Trick asked.

"No. I thought you guys were handling the breaking and entering."

"Sylvester prefers to call it visiting and pilfering. And it was his responsibility to carry those spells. I didn't think we'd get trapped and teleported to Sheol."

We should have prepared for this eventuality, just in case.

She wasn't ready to die.

I could try prying the bars apart. I have gloves in my bag.

But while Seraphina was strong, she couldn't boast the brute force needed. Her fighting skills lay in her speed and agility, not her muscle mass.

The sound of a bell chiming loudly made her ears pound. Looking around wildly, she asked, "Where is that coming from?"

"It's the signal that a Hell-lord has arrived in another Hell-lord's realm."

The noise was nearly deafening. *I guess it ensures they can't sneak up on each other.*

She focused on Trick, noting the slight pinch of pain in his features. "Do you think Hades has come for us?"

"The timing seems coincidental, but Hades can't get us out. And he can't really admit he hired us to steal from Lucifer in the first place."

Seraphina wanted to refute the demon's logic, but it was sound.

"Hades can't get you out, but I can."

Seraphina glancing sharply towards the voice, which had come from within the cell.

A tall Asian woman stood there, her jet-black hair swept up in a loose bun with a tiny paper umbrella perched on the side. She wore nothing but a bikini, sarong and flip-flops. She was beautiful, with fine features and a regal bearing, but it was her power that hummed through the cell.

What is she?

Whoever this woman was, she was someone to avoid.

"*Asha?*" Trick said in a strangled voice.

"The one and only." She twirled a pair of sunglasses in her hand.

Trick's eyes roved over the newcomer. "You do realize you can't teleport out of here."

"That's why I brought this." A bag appeared in her hands.

"I'm sorry, but who is this?" Seraphina turned to Trick.

"This is Asha Himm."

Hades' PA.

Asha shot Trick a glare. "And I'm currently meant to be on holiday. You're messing with my time off, and I am serious about my annual leave."

He held out his hands, palms up. "Ooops?"

She sighed. "Follow me."

Turning to the bars, she studied them for a moment, before rummaging in her bag. "This should work." She threw a fistful of powder toward the entrance. The scent of hot, sizzling metal rose in the air, competing with the stench of rotten eggs. The bars disintegrated within seconds.

"*That* is going to be noticeable." Trick frowned.

"You want me to break you out or not?" Asha demanded, hands on hips.

"We want out," Seraphina said quickly.

Hades' PA turned back to the steaming pile of molten metal. "Thought so." Stepping over the debris, she waved at them to follow. Out in the corridor, Asha looked left, then right, before counting on her fingers, and pursing her lips.

"Do you know where you're going?" Trick queried.

"Of course." She drew her chin up haughtily, before staring at her toes.

Trick came up next to Seraphina, and leaned down to whisper, "This does not fill me with confidence."

His breath sent a small shiver down her spine, her skin coming alive, craving his touch.

That isn't good.

"I heard that," Asha said. "We go left."

They had only made it four steps before the Elock guard thundered down the hall. The demon skidded to a stop in front of them, dark eyes wide in his sunken face. Without warning, Asha lashed out with a side kick, breaking the demon's nose in a crunch of cartilage. She followed the blow with three well-placed punches, knocking the creature out cold. The Elock demon crashed to the floor in a scream of armor.

"We should kill it," Seraphina said into the silence that followed.

"It is a he," Trick muttered. "And if you think Lucifer

will be angry now, wait till you kill one of his guards."

"The guild master is right," Asha said. "We leave him as is."

"But he'll recognize us."

Trick shook his head. "Elock demons don't have the best memories. We can chance it."

All her training rebelled at the thought of leaving a witness alive, but she kept her protests to herself. This Asha woman and Trick had been living and working in Hell for hundreds of years, no doubt. They knew the protocols better than she did.

They stepped over the Elock's body and hurried down the corridor. Shadows seemed to stretch and reach for them as they approached the end.

Asha turned to them. "Stay close. Once we get out of the dungeons, I should be able to teleport you."

"I can teleport," Trick said, almost defensively.

Asha looked at him askance. "It takes a fair bit of power to get out of these wards, but you can try."

Instead of looking put out by the insult, Trick appeared contemplative. *No doubt assessing how much more powerful Asha is, compared to him.*

The few times Seraphina had met Trick previously, she hadn't thought he was that...well, intelligent. Handsome, yes; brutal, of course. But she had been lax in assuming he didn't have a keen mind under that pretty exterior. You didn't get to run—and stay running—a mercenary guild with just brute force.

At the end of the corridor, the shadows swallowed them. For a moment, she struggled to breathe—malevolent evil swirled in the air currents. Then she was through the swarm of darkness, and in a well-lit stairwell.

"Where now?" Trick asked.

"We go up. But be careful."

"Wait." Seraphina withdrew a small dagger, and sliced her forearm, hissing slightly at the pain. It took a lot of magic to create invisibility spells, but she could manage two in a day. That would be it, though.

She'd be almost useless after.

She smeared blood in a glyph on her chest.

"Oh, that's great! I need you to teach me that spell." Asha's eyes searched the small area, homing in on Seraphina's location by the blood that appeared on Trick's shirt before he too vanished.

Seraphina ignored the hard muscle tone under her fingertip.

Turning to Asha, she said, "Your turn." She then drew the glyph on the demon's bare belly. Cold zapped up her arm at the contact, the chill almost painful. Once the spell was in place, she jerked her arm back. "What are you?"

"I'm a cambion."

And I am an archangel.

"We're still going to need to see each other," Asha said, and Seraphina could hear her sorting through her bag. "Here."

A fumbling hand reached out and poked Seraphina with something. Grabbing the item, she realized it was a makeup case. Opening it, she saw it contained the same dark powder as Sylvester had used earlier.

"You brought Clear Sight?"

"I've got all sorts of goodies in here."

Seraphina smeared it on her eyelids, before handing it to Trick, whose gaze, she could now see, was skittering about the room. His hand engulfed hers for a brief moment, before he applied the enchantment.

"Okay. I see everyone."

"As do I," Seraphina said.

"Why don't more people have these?" Trick asked.

Asha stowed the case away in her bag. "Because they are super expensive. You just put on about five hundred bucks worth each. Now, we need to get up to the main floor, so move quickly, quietly, and follow my steps."

They took to the staircase, plastering themselves to the side when a guard clonked past. They were approaching the third landing when a shout rolled up through the passageway.

"You think they found the guard?" Trick whispered.

"Sounds like it," Asha replied. "Let's go."

They took off up the stairs at a sprint, Seraphina following at the rear; she had been one of Heaven's quickest fliers, and she hadn't been slow on foot, either, but she still had to work a little to keep up with the others.

They're fast. I'd enjoy racing them on flat ground one day.

More guards filed past them, spears in hand, their deep voices rumbling in their native language. Seraphina pressed close to the wall, as if she was trying to merge with it.

Eventually, they made it out the stairwell, coming to a stop in a small chamber, which was half-filled with guards talking madly to each other. Asha moved close, until the three of them were huddled together. "We need to get out of here."

Seraphina and Trick nodded.

They dodged through the crowd, passed beneath an archway, and moved into a wide brick hall decorated with suits of armor. Oily, nausea-inducing magic wafted from the displays, and peering at the closest one, she saw the hollow sockets of a skull beneath the helmet. Glancing at the others, she realized they all contained skeletons.

Necromancy.

Revulsion raced through her. To desecrate the dead in such a way...

"Come." Asha grabbed Seraphina's arm and dragged her to a small alcove. The contact was freezing and she pulled away as soon as she could.

Once hidden in the small side area, Hades' PA nodded at Trick, who closed his eyes in concentration. He shook his head.

No luck on the teleportation, then.

"Give me your hands," Asha said.

Reaching out, Seraphina fought a wince as the cold bit into her burned palms.

Their surroundings changed, morphing into a deep forest, with a small cottage in the background.

Asha bent over at the waist, panting. "We're out."

Drumbeats filled the air. Seraphina pressed her aching palms over her ears. "What is *that*?"

"Lucifer just closed the realm," Trick said, eyes wide. He focused on her, expression solemn. "We're stuck in Sheol."

CHAPTER 24

Trick was a dead man standing.

Lucifer had locked Sheol down. No one out. No one in.

Fuck. Fuckity, fuck, fuck.

This could go on for days, weeks, even, and they only had three-and-a-bit days left on Hades' deadline. The thing was, Hades didn't bluff. So, if the god said the price of failure was death, then it was really was death.

And Trick didn't want to die.

"Lucifer's shut the realm? He can do that?" Seraphina bit her lip, then glared at the treed landscape around them, as if it were to blame.

"Yup." Asha ran a hand over her cheek. "All the Hell-lords can, although Satan has only ever done it three times, and Hades once. Lucifer tends to do it every other decade."

"You think it's because he found out we escaped?" Trick asked.

"I would think so." Asha whipped out her cell and tapped at the screen. "He won't know who he had in his cells, so he'll be paranoid it was a spy. Hades says a guard came to deliver the news that someone had been transported to the prison, but had escaped without being seen. Lucifer was with him at the time. Seems his face was priceless." She raised an eyebrow. "You're lucky Hades finds this amusing."

"He's the one who demanded we go on this mission." And it had been nothing but a disaster ever since.

"Yeah, you have fun telling him that when it goes even more pear-shaped."

"I will." Not that he'd come out the other end of that chat alive. But at the rate they were going, they wouldn't live to see the end of the week, anyway.

Seraphina kicked at the dirt. "Where to now? Are we staying at that cottage?"

Trick spun on his heel, taking in the small building amid the trees. "Is that a *Wayfarer's Hut*?"

He'd heard of them, of course. But he had never seen one in person. Safe havens within Hell, they were warded with anti-violence spells and were places of refuge for the weary traveler. They were legendary, and didn't just appear to anyone.

"It sure is." Asha grinned. "But you aren't staying here."

"Why not?"

"This is my beach resort; you guys can find your own."

Beach resort?

There wasn't an ocean within sight, and the soil beneath their feet certainly lacked the glamor of beach sand.

"Kicking us out, Asha?" Trick asked.

"More like not inviting you to stay. I had to leave my tropical paradise to get your ass out of there, and now I am stuck in Sheol. You guys can sort yourselves out now. You're work, and I'm on holidays."

She spun on her heel, and walked toward the hut, her hips swaying beneath her sarong.

"Is she really leaving us here?" Seraphina demanded.

"Looks like it."

"Can she do that?"

"She can do anything she wants," Trick muttered. Working for Hades, she was pretty much untouchable. And she *was* a demi-goddess of some kind.

"Where do we go?"

Trick thought through his list of contacts in Sheol. "I know a place."

Seraphina's mouth closed in a thin line, but she didn't argue.

"Thanks, Asha!" Trick shouted to the goddess' retreating back. "Pleasure doing business with you, as always!"

She gave them a flippant wave, then knocked on the Wayfarer's Hut's door.

I really want to see inside there.

But Asha had made it clear they were to go their own way. Taking a deep breath, he placed a hand on Seraphina's arm and focused on their new location.

They re-appeared outside the Casa de los Condenados.

The home of the damned.

The Casa de los Condenados was a popular destination for tourists, and Trick's favorite watering hole. They sold information here like they did beer. The

Human Realm was also so close, you could almost smell the pollution in the air, and see the neighboring street through the hazy barrier.

Letting go of Seraphina's arm, he strode toward the bar's entrance.

"What is this place?" she asked, eyes scanning the building.

It looked more like an old manor house than a tavern, complete with three stories and a gabled slate roof. But inside, the ground floor was a typical bar. A long counter traversed the length of the room, with shelves containing all kinds of alcohol behind it. Round tables were scattered throughout the open chamber, which had a polished concrete floor—easier to hose down after a fight.

The bar was packed, filled from end to end with a variety of demons, and the occasional human. *Probably going to be someone's snack, later.* One of the bartenders was sweeping up a tinkling pile of a broken glass as they entered. The Foraci demon flicked a glance their way, before returning her attention to the broom. She had tattoos covering her right cheek and descending down her neck: a Scryer. One of the most rare and powerful of her kind.

Seraphina frowned at the demon, then bent to pick up something near her feet. She pocketed it before Trick could see what she'd found. *Damnit.* He'd have to check it out another time.

He approached the bar, the angel close at his heels. He was searching for the owner, when a large shadow fell over them.

"Now who might this be?" A high, accented voice asked.

Trick glanced over his shoulder. The shadow belonged to Lamar, the bar's owner, and a Djinn; someone you did not mess with, unless you were powerful enough to take him on. Lamar, however, currently only had eyes for Seraphina. In fact, his expression was a little glazed, as if stunned by her unnatural beauty.

I know the feeling, buddy.

"What can I do for you?" Lamar gave her a broad smile, flexing his arms to show off his immense muscles. Then the Djinn sniffed the air and stiffened, his eyes turning to pools of flame. "Angel," he spat.

Seraphina drew herself up, her own eyes going wide. "Djinn."

Angels and Djinn were cousins, of a sort. Not that angels liked to admit as much, and the Djinn had grown to resent their Heavenly brethren over the millennia.

"What are you doing here?" Lamar demanded.

"Looking for a place to stay. And for the owner of this." From her pocket, she withdrew a single feather. It was the color of a crow's wing, shiny with health, and delicate.

The Djinn snorted, his eyes returning to their orange hue. "It's a bird's."

Trick reached out and touched the feather, stiffening at its residual power. This was an angel feather—and not just any angel's. This belonged to someone powerful. But he had never heard of an angel with black wings before.

How intriguing.

"It's an angel's. Whose is it?" Seraphina demanded.

"It's no one's. Give it to me."

"No." Seraphina closed her fist over the tiny treasure.

"Then leave." The Djinn clenched his jaw.

Trick stepped between them, before the confrontation could turn ugly. "Lamar."

The Djinn focused on him and paled slightly. "Mr. Trick."

"My colleague and I are searching for accommodation. Can you give us a room?"

The bar owner tried to look past him to Seraphina. "Eyes on me, Lamar. A room. Do you have one?"

The Djinn swallowed. "We are booked up. With Lucifer closing down the realm, I have a sudden influx of guests."

"So, you don't have a room?" Trick's voice was a silky lash.

The Djinn winced. "I have one."

"Then we will take it."

Lamar straightened his shoulders. "Only if she gives the feather back."

Interesting, that the Djinn was so invested in that tiny piece of fluff. But right now, Trick had to focus on finding a safe place for the night. If they had to camp, it would be a rough time, especially when the native denizens of Hell loved to consume angelic flesh.

"Give him the feather, Seraphina."

She shot him a betrayed glance.

Lamar held out his hand, wiggling his large fingers impatiently.

With a reluctant sigh—and a glare—she placed the feather in the waiting palm. "I would like to speak to the feather's owner."

Lamar shook his head. "Trust me, angel. They don't want to speak to you."

Hurt flashed across Seraphina's face before she could mask it.

Does she know who owns the feather? What is going on?

"Here." The Djinn handed Trick a key. "Room seven, second floor, at the end of the corridor. It has its own bathroom. I recommend you keep your angel on a tight leash."

Seraphina hissed.

"Excellent." Trick took gentle hold of her arm and pulled her away from the Djinn.

"But—"

"Later."

He herded Seraphina across the bar's ground floor, to the other end of the room, where a staircase led upstairs. She planted her feet at the base of the stairs and crossed her arms.

"I am not going up there. I need to learn more about the feather."

"Not right now you don't." Annoyed, Trick whipped out a hand, touching her arm quickly and teleported them to the second floor.

Scowling, she jerked away from his hold. "I am going back downstairs."

"Sweetheart, if you want to piss Lamar off, go right ahead. But he's a Djinn and he owns this place. Do you really want to mess with him?"

Eventually, she ground out, "No."

"Then come on."

Room seven was at the end of the hall. Opening the door, he saw it was a decent size, with a desk, fridge and bathroom. The only problem? There was just one bed.

I am not sleeping on the floor.
"Dibs on the bed!"

CHAPTER 25

Mother *fucker*.

Yael rubbed the bridge of his nose, and stared at the fading, shimmering barrier. He stood at the back of Lafitte's Blacksmith Shop Bar; the stale smell of alcohol mingled with the sticky humidity of the Human Realm.

How had that not worked?

He'd opened a Devilsgate, and then *bam*! he'd been smacked in the face by a brick wall and deposited here. He could even see the faintest shimmer of a manor house in Sheol, the Casa de los Condenados now just a mirage against the brickwork wall of the bar's courtyard. But his quarry was stubbornly in Hell, while he wasn't.

I did everything right. I should be standing in front of that bar, right now.

Instead, he was stuck in New Orleans with a sore face.

Glancing around the empty Blacksmith's courtyard, Yael breathed a sigh of relief. At eight in the morning, the bar was empty of patrons and staff. No one would have noticed his sudden appearance, and hopefully wouldn't see his equally sudden departure. Although, this was

NOLA; from what he'd heard, that kind of thing was par for the course here.

Reaching into his pocket, he withdrew another bag of gate-dust, and threw some into the air. It shimmered with magic, before falling to the ground in a spray of expensive dirt. *Very* expensive dirt.

What the actual fuck?

Yael grabbed his phone from his back pocket, then hesitated. He hadn't told Raze or Azrael where he'd gone, or even that he'd left. Raze was used to his absences, and he didn't trust Azrael like he used to, not after he'd shacked up with that sociopathic cambion, Dru.

Couldn't Azrael see that she was a disaster waiting to happen?

Skies, you could argue she had *already* happened. Azrael would never get back into Heaven mated to a demon—a cambion, at that. And as for Z...nope. Yael wouldn't go there. The other Dart had already suffered so much, and to then be mated to the queen of the Mortus, no less...

Z was doomed already, no matter that he had kept his wings.

Unlike those two, Yael did not plan on spending the rest of his eternity on this dust ball *or* in Hell.

You could tell Raze.

Raze was logical, sound, and reliable. Although, why the angel had accumulated immense wealth in the Human Realm while still an angel was anybody's guess. But angels could have some strange habits, and Yael figured that money-making was one of Raze's.

Yael liked to collect garrotes.

And use them.

Right now, he had to track down his quarry, which would prove difficult when they were in Sheol and he was in the Human Realm. He'd heard whispers of a black-winged angel, and he had wanted to see this individual for himself.

There was every chance it was Dina, his former captain.

But there was every other chance it was another fallen angel, one that had eventually grown powerful enough to regenerate their wings. It was meant to be impossible, but Yael had come to understand that the archangels were not all that forthcoming with facts, or even the truth. You could lie without actually uttering a falsehood.

And if there was a fallen angel that powerful...it was an ace he could keep up his sleeve. If all else failed, and the Darts couldn't retrieve all three pieces of the Heart, then he could present the angel's head to the archangels, on the proviso that he was reinstated in Heaven. To Yael, nothing mattered more than ascending back to his former life.

Being wingless and less significant than before was not acceptable. He had had a life back in Heaven; family, friends, and the occasional lover. *What would Mother and Father think of me now?*

They would be bowed with shame, that's what.

His parents had always wanted him to be more: more powerful, more intelligent, more *everything*. His whole life, he'd disappointed them. He'd developed silver filaments in his wings rather than gold. He'd been second in his scholarly training, rather than first. When he'd been awarded his place in the Darts, they had finally shown a dash of pleasure in his achievements, but they'd been disappointed he was not the captain.

Now, everything they'd thought about him would be true.

He *was* a failure.

Not if I can find this angel.

If it was Dina, and he saved her, the Darts would be whole once more, even with Z living in Hell. Z was on their side when it came to finding all the pieces of Heaven's Heart. He would step up when needed. And Dina was so powerful that finding the other fragments of the Heart would be a piece of cake.

But he just had to get into Hell to find her.

There is still Seraphina. She might have some contacts.

Half driven by guilt, half by frustration, he still couldn't think of Seraphina without anger filling him. She'd shown him yet again why he wasn't the angel his parents had dreamed of, because she'd been willing to sacrifice her soul for the Darts, for Z.

Yael had been desperate to avoid such a fate.

Still, he trusted her.

She would do right by the Darts, and wanted to get back into Heaven just as much as he did. And she wasn't angry at him for being a dick; she'd messaged him earlier.

Okay. He'd call her, then Raze, to see if they knew why the spell hadn't worked.

The phone rang for a few moments before a male voice answered. "Seraphina's phone."

Had she been hurt? Kidnapped? Why was some stranger taking her calls? Yael clenched his free hand. "Who is this?"

"Who are you?"

"I asked first."

"I asked second."

Who was this fucking moron?

Seraphina shouted in the background. "Give me the phone!"

"You didn't say the magic word!"

"Give me the phone, please."

"Fine."

A rustling of cloth, then, "Hello?"

"Seraphina?"

"Yael?"

"Who the Hell was that?"

"Trick. My new boss."

That still didn't explain why the guy was answering her phone, but at least it meant she was okay. *Maybe he's screening her calls.* If he did, that was fucking scummy. "He's an asshole."

"You got that right. Now, how can I help you?"

"Hey! I heard that!" Trick called out.

He had damned good hearing. Yael would have to go and research what type of demon this ass was. Once he knew, it would be easier to kill the bastard.

"I just tried to get into Sheol, but was knocked back. Have you heard of a reason why that would happen?"

Silence, more rustling of cloth and then, "Why were you trying to get into Sheol?"

"Just doing some research."

"Don't go meeting Lucifer, Yael. It's not worth it."

"I want nothing to do with Lucifer."

And that was one hundred percent the truth. He liked living.

Rumor had it, that when angels fell, Lucifer's realm was the place to go; that he had a soft spot for his brethren. But Yael had also heard that some angels who went to the Hell-lord were never heard of again.

"Lucifer has locked Sheol down. No one in, no one out."

Fuck.

"Any idea when it will reopen?"

"No."

"Thanks."

"No worries."

He didn't want to ask, but... "Is it all going okay? The whole slave thing?"

She paused. "As well as can be expected."

That was a non-answer.

"Be careful," she said, when he didn't respond.

"Will do." But the lie tasted ill on his tongue.

CHAPTER 26

Seraphina threw the phone on the green floral-patterned bedspread.

Why is Yael trying to get into Sheol?

She resisted the urge to text him back to find out. Yael was relatively private, and she didn't want to intrude. Plus, he could very well be doing a job for the Falling Star, and it was best if she knew nothing about their dealings for the time being.

If Lucifer doesn't open up Sheol within the next day or so, it won't matter what you do or don't know. You'll be dead.

"What do you mean, Metcalf ate the cat?" Trick sat on the floor in the corner of the room, knees bent up and shouting into his cell, which was plugged into the wall to charge. "We don't even *have* a cat!"

She didn't hear the reply, but smiled as the demon ran a tired hand down his disbelieving face. The moment he'd realized there was cell reception, he'd called the guild to check in. Like the place would fall down if he didn't.

"You bought a Montsorrean larval cat? *And* you let it

out of your room?"

What on earth was a Montsorrean larval cat? It didn't sound like a regular cat breed. Was it one of those hairless varieties, that looked like men's...well, testicles?

Poor things.

Cats really looked better with their fur.

"Oh, it was on a leash. That makes it *so much better.* Those things grow up to become the size of rhinos!"

Seraphina had never heard of a cat that big before. Not even tigers grew that large. *It must be a Hell-species.*

No wonder Trick sounded like he was having a heart-attack.

"I am not going to add the cost of the cat to Metcalf's debt. Are you kidding me?"

She placed her backpack on the bed next to her phone and rummaged through it for some spare clothes. They would have to flip a coin to see who got to take the bed, and who had the floor, because she was *not* going to share it. He'd already left enough of a mark on her, she didn't need to add to it.

While Trick attended to administration duties, she was going to have a shower. After finding what she needed, she zipped the bag back up and threw it over her shoulder.

"And I am not going to make Metcalf apologize! You work for a goddamn mercenary guild. You should have looked after your pet better!"

Seraphina headed into the adjoining bathroom and locked the door behind her. She needn't have bothered, though, because when she emerged ten minutes later, Trick was still hunched in the corner, although he was now tugging at the golden strands of his hair as he talked.

"You want him to join the guild *now*?"

He didn't even look up as she puttered around.

"I am stuck in Sheol. Can it wait?"

He was silent for a moment.

"Fine. A week. Give me a week. You do know the other guild members are going to lose their shit over this?"

Curious despite herself, Seraphina decided that they needed some food and drink. That way she couldn't blatantly eavesdrop. *It's none of my business, and I shouldn't care. I am not going to be around long enough to have to know anything about how the guild works.*

Although, if there is *a new guild member, I should be aware of that.* She could ask Trick about it.

Slipping downstairs, she caught Lamar's eye as she entered the taproom. From behind the bar, he jerked his head at her, indicating she should come on over. She shoved her way through the crowd, confusion and curiosity following in her wake as demons tried to work out what she was.

"Lamar." Her gaze dropped to the pocket where he'd stashed the black feather. It had belonged to an angel, no matter what the Djinn said.

It might belong to Dina.

Not that she had any evidence that Dina could be black-winged; she'd had almost pure silver wings back in Heaven. But Z's had changed upon entering Hell, so it was possible their former captain's had as well.

It gave her hope, to think that Dina was still alive.

Seraphina telepathically called out to her, but there was no response. There hadn't been for seven months, since the Heart had been stolen.

"I said to stay in your room," Lamar growled.

Be polite. It's not his fault he's a Djinn.

Wow. That was super racist, she realized. And it was just the kind of thinking that would be frowned upon in Heaven. Not the racist bit, but the part where she was forgiving of the fact that the Djinn was a Djinn.

The archangels did not like that they were related to this particular class of demon, and were quite vociferous about their views.

"Just some dinner and a drink, if that's okay?" she asked.

Lamar stared at her for a few moments. "Fine. I'll bring it up. You a vegan? I've heard angels don't eat meat."

"I'd prefer not to, but will have whatever you prepare."

He frowned, his orange eyes swirling with flames. "You being nice to me won't make me give you the feather back."

"I wouldn't have thought otherwise."

Something almost like respect flashed in his eyes.

While it was true she desperately wanted the feather, it didn't really matter if she had it or not. She'd seen it, touched it, knew its power. Finding the owner was more important. Having the feather would make it easier, but then, nothing had been easy since they'd fallen.

A demon bumped her shoulder playfully with his. "Hey, beautiful. Come here often?"

She stared at him. He was about the same height as her, with two long horns gracing the top of his head. Other than that, he appeared human.

"No, this is the first time."

The demon eyed her lecherously. "Really—"

Lamar's large hand slapped down on the bar. "This one is not for you."

"But Lamar—"

"No." The Djinn switched his fiery gaze to Seraphina. "Go back upstairs. Now."

She nodded, turned on her heel and left. Whispers trailed after her as she moved, but she ignored them, focusing on the stairs. *Do not grab your knife. Do not.* But some of the looks that followed her were filled with barely bridled lust. It made her wary.

I am not a plaything to be toyed with.

Now I understand how human women feel. To be looked upon as if they were cows, ready for the slaughter.

Except in her case, she'd be the one doing the killing.

Reaching the stairs, she let out a little sigh of relief, and ascended them quickly. If a fight broke out over her, and she killed a demon in self-defense, she had a feeling that Lamar would blame her. And Trick had been very set on them staying here, not somewhere else in Sheol. She didn't want him annoyed at her for losing their accommodation.

Plus, I don't want to camp in Hell.

She worried that the longer she stayed, the more corrupt she would become. The more…human.

Trick was still on the phone when she entered, so she cleared off the small table in their room and went hunting for cutlery. There was none. *Do they expect us to eat with our hands?*

In the background, Trick groaned. "No, Errant. Tell Mim that she can't order six hundred steaks just because there's a sale on at Costco. Same goes for pumpkin pies.

We'd be eating the stuff for months. You know half of the guild won't touch them because they've got a vegetable in the name."

There was a knock on the door, and, dagger in hand, she went to answer it. It was just Lamar, burdened with a tray of plates and glasses, as well as two jugs, one she presumed filled with water. It was either that, or vodka.

"Here." The Djinn shoved the tray at her.

She returned the knife to its sheath and took the food. "That was quick."

"Didn't want to give you a reason to come back downstairs. There's already bets on what species you are, and if you're edible."

Seraphina shot him a bland smile. "If they try anything on me, they die."

"That's why you're staying up here. I don't need you killing off my clientele. What he—" Lamar nodded his head in Trick's direction "—is doing with you, I don't know."

"I'm his latest employee."

"Uhh." The Djinn flicked a glance at the bed.

"Mercenary employee. Not whore."

"Hey." Lamar held his hands up. "It's a noble profession. I'll leave you to it." The Djinn backed away a couple steps, and she closed the door on his smirk.

Strangely, she felt no horror that the Djinn thought she was Trick's lover.

She set the tray down on the table, listening to Trick argue with and cajole his guild members into better moods. *He cares.* She didn't know what drove that emotion—probably greed—but he seemed invested in keeping his slaves and employees content.

It was more than she could say for some angels she'd once known.

You can't order someone to be happy.

Although she'd known angels who had tried to do just that.

She was one of them, but the person she'd been instructing had been herself. *If I told myself I was happy enough, then I believed I was happy.* It was only after she'd left Heaven that she'd realized what a lie that had been.

Seraphina lifted the cloches on the tray, checking to see what meals lay hidden beneath. A steak, mashed potato and some peas lay on one plate, while steaming pasta served with snow peas and roasted pumpkin was on another. It looked rather delicious. She poured herself a glass of water, which she drank quickly, then picked up the second jug: 'Djinn Spiced Mead'.

It sounded harmless enough.

She poured herself a glass, admiring the amber liquid, and the flecks of cinnamon and nutmeg churning within its bubbly depths. Next to the plates was a paper bag filled with cutlery. *Excellent.* She pulled up the only chair in the room, sat down, and dug into the meal. The first sip of the mead had her closing her eyes in bliss. Warm spices floated on her tongue, while the liquid bubbled gently. She swallowed, and heat bled through her, loosening her limbs, making her languid.

This is better than the shower.

Before she knew it, half the bowl of pasta was gone, and her glass was drained. She poured herself a second as Trick hung up the phone.

"Oh, you got food. Great, I'm starving."

She handed him the plate and a knife and fork. He

looked at the table with its limited space, shrugged, and sat on the floor at the end of the bed. Somehow, Trick managed to eat the meal with excellent table manners, even though he used his lap as a plate.

"Everything okay back at the guild? You were on the phone a while." Damnit, she hadn't intended to ask. Downing the rest of the mead, she poured herself another glass, enjoying the relaxation that soaked her limbs.

He paused, fork halfway to his mouth. "Everything is as to be expected."

"Cat-eating is a normal thing?"

Trick snorted, the mashed potato he'd just put in his mouth spraying everywhere. He wiped away the mess with a napkin. "No, Metcalf eating other demon's pets isn't normal, because I have a no pet policy. For that very reason."

"I see."

He shot her a look. "Don't go getting any ideas."

"I had no intention of getting a pet." She took another sip of mead.

I feel wonderful.

She packed her plate away, stood, and carried her glass over to the bed. Reclining on the soft mattress, she sighed in ecstasy. This was the best she had felt in *years*.

Trick looked over his shoulder. "What are you doing?"

"Lying down."

"But I called dibs on the bed. It's mine."

"What is 'dibs'?" She pushed herself up on her elbows.

"It's a proprietary claim. You call it first, you get it. You're on the floor."

That system wasn't fair—especially if not everyone

involved knew it existed. "You're not using the bed."

"I will be," he muttered.

"But you aren't now."

Grumbling, he returned to his meal.

She sank into the mattress as Trick finished his meal. He was putting his plate back on the table when she said, "I think you should move my brand."

The crockery rattled. "I should what now?"

"Move my brand."

His eyes flittered around the room. "Another time."

"I'm free at the moment."

"Really, we can do it another time. I'd have to touch your lips again."

The thought of kissing him made her breasts tingle and the heat from the mead settle deep in her stomach. "Excellent. Let's do it now."

Trick swallowed. "Uh..."

CHAPTER 27

Seraphina splayed out on the bed, her fingers clutching a glass filled with amber liquid, and her eyes warm pools of desire.

Wait. Desire? Why is she looking at me like that?

Maybe it was the giddiness that came with survival? Knowing that they had managed to escape from the Tower of Tortures with their limbs—and lives—intact?

"Come on. It's just a quick kiss. That way I don't have to wear lipstick all the time."

I don't have any good reason to refuse her. Other than the fact that if he kissed her while she was on that bed, he'd want to do a whole lot more with her. And that would be bad. Very bad.

But it would feel so good.

And who was to say she'd want to do more? Maybe she just wanted the brand shifted? He'd never do anything she didn't want, so if he just changed the brand's location, then no harm done.

Right.

He could do this.

"Where do you want the mark to go?" Trick asked, standing.

She shot him a coy look—*strange*—and ran her hand down her torso, resting it on the side of her belly. "Here." Then her hand slid lower, to stop on her thigh. "Or maybe here."

He bit the inside of his cheek. Great. Stomach or leg. Both were eminently sensible choices; they could be revealed when desired, and hidden otherwise. No one ever need know she was a blood slave if she didn't want them to.

Walking over to the bed, he sat on the edge, looking down at her. She was beauty personified, from her gleaming dark skin, to her full lips, and molten eyes.

Ignore that. Do the job.

"You need to lift your shirt, so I can reach your stomach."

"Of course."

She raised the cloth, until the underside of her bra was exposed. It was just white cotton, but...

Wow.

Eyes away. Eyes away.

It was too late. He'd seen it. *What's seen cannot be unseen.* And it was making his cock hard, his breathing a little wonky. His hands itched to touch her, to trace over the smooth planes of her skin, to delve into her hair.

Get a grip.

Taking a deep breath, he leaned forward, ignoring the throb of his cock. Quickly, he pressed his lips to hers, drawing on the magic deep within the slave bond. He then placed a hand on her belly—*so smooth*—transferring the mark there. Once the spell had taken, he pulled away, mind already hazing with lust.

Done.

Seraphina moaned in protest and pulled his head back down to her mouth. Their lips met in a clash of passion, her tongue darting out to meet his. He groaned, a deep, guttural sound, and pressed his body against hers, reveling in the feel of her. She undulated underneath him, angling so that her core pressed against his erection.

Hell, that feels good.

Too good.

His hand slid up her torso, and over to cup one of her breasts. It filled his palm completely, like her body had been made just for him. The thought jolted through the lust pounding in his blood, and he pulled away from her.

"Seraphina, we should stop."

"Mmm. More." She jerked his head back down, her strength incredible. She tasted of spices and beer.

Wait.

"Sera, what was in your drink?"

She kept kissing him, even though he had angled his head away. She nibbled his jaw, while her hands massaged down his back, heading toward his ass. "Spiced mead."

"What kind of spiced mead?"

"Djinn."

"Right." With a heave, he rolled away and onto the other side of the bed. She pounced, trying to pin him down, and a small wrestling match ensued. By the time he'd freed himself, he was sweaty and ready to explode. He quickly dived off the bed to stand next to the wall.

She pouted, reaching from him.

"I need to have a shower," he blurted, and bolted for

the bathroom. He locked the door behind him and pressed himself against the wooden panel.

Breathe.

It was hard to concentrate while his throbbing cock yelled abuse at him for running away. But she wasn't sober, was in fact, very, very drunk. He wasn't about to take advantage of her, even though his willpower had been fading with every drugging kiss.

She'd hate me for it.

Not to mention he'd hate himself, too.

Trick was many things, but a rapist, he was not.

Who needs to force when they flock to me like bees to honey, anyway?

Well, they'd all flocked *except* Dru, and now Seraphina.

Giving himself a shake, he stripped off his shirt and pants, leaving them in a pile on the floor. He would have to brave the room again at some point, so he could get fresh clothes. Hopefully, she'd be asleep by then.

Turning on the shower, he waited for it to warm up. He stepped into the spray and gave a hiss of pleasure as the water flowed over him. It felt good—like he hadn't had a shower in months. His erection bobbed, still angry at him for denying it.

Gently taking it in his fist, he ran his hand up and down the length, his mind turning to Seraphina's mouth, her breasts. He was in the middle of picturing what her core would look like when the bathroom door burst open.

He spun around and slipped, landing on the floor of the bath with a crash, the curtain slithering off the railing to fall on his face. Pain burst through his hip; he'd be bruised for a few hours. He shoved the shower curtain away so he could peer around it.

Dear lord.

Seraphina was naked, except for a necklace on which hung a small silvery feather.

Every inch of her glorious form was exposed for him to see, and he couldn't get enough of it.

"What are you doing?" It came out more like a squeak than a demand. He took a deep breath, but all that did was highlight the scent of her: ambrosia.

"I thought I could do with a shower."

He stood slowly, keeping the shower curtain up over his belly. "You had one earlier."

She gave him a scorching look. "But I feel dirty."

Gods help me.

He shook his head as she stepped forward. "There isn't enough room for two people."

"Let's find out." She eyed his exposed chest like it was dessert.

He tugged the shower curtain higher. "Let's not."

"But—"

Struggling, he managed to step out the bath and keep the curtain around him. He then pushed her toward the door, careful to keep a hand on her shoulder. "You're drunk. You need to sleep."

"No, the last thing I need is sleep."

"That's where you're wrong."

"Why won't you kiss me?"

"I already did."

"Didn't you like it?" Something almost like hurt flashed across her face. Then she twined her arms around his neck.

"Sure did. But it's time for sleep." He somehow

managed to get the both of them out of the bathroom. What was he going to do? She was persistent, strong, and his willpower wasn't all that wonderful when it came to resisting her.

He scurried out from under her arms and grabbed his pack. She grabbed his ass, her hand sliding over the shower curtain. Her jerked upright, bag in hand. Seraphina placed a series of kisses down the back of his neck, while her hand worked to loosen the plastic around his waist.

Trick fumbled the bag open, found what he needed, and undid a small plastic ziplock packet. He tried to pour only a pinch of the brilliant blue powder onto his hand, but the angel knocked him, and a teaspoon's worth pooled there. He was about to pour half back into the bag, when her hand snaked around the front of the curtain.

No time.

Spinning around, he blew the powder directly into her face.

For a moment, nothing happened.

"What—?"

Then Seraphina's eyes rolled back, and she collapsed. Asleep.

Carefully, he lowered her to the ground, and checked her airway and pulse. All okay. He turned her into the recovery position and stood, head bowed in relief. Then he straightened, pulled the shower curtain free, and went back into the bathroom to hang it up. He turned off the shower and examined the bruise on his hip: already black and purple, it would fade in the next hour. It still hurt.

Returning to the room, he gathered up Seraphina's clothing, and popped it in a pile on her bag, wondering what he should do about the naked angel. She lay on the ground, every superb angle of her visible.

I should put her to bed.

She was going to feel embarrassed and sore tomorrow morning, he'd bet on that.

Should I dress her?

Yes, but putting clothes on a dead weight was hard work. He decided on her panties, and then figured she'd be under a bedspread for the remainder of the night. Once he'd tucked her in, he grabbed some pillows from the bed, found a spare blanket, and set up a little place for him to sleep on the floor—between the bed and the door.

Now, to finish my shower.

He was done in a minute or two, his erection long gone, thankfully. He dressed and climbed under his blanket. *At least the floor is carpeted.* Retrieving his tablet, he replied to a few emails, and read the latest from Hades, which outlined the terms of their current job.

The god had underlined 'Failure will result in death if task not complete in a week'.

Asshole.

Tucking the tablet away, he rolled onto his side, staring at the door.

If he were to tell anyone that he'd had a beautiful angel climbing all over him—and that he refused her advances—no one would believe him.

And you know what, I like it that way.

Trick fell asleep, a small smile tilting the corners of his lips.

CHAPTER 28

Seraphina's head pounded, her mouth dry as desert sands.

What happened?

Raising a hand to her forehead, she frowned when she realized she wasn't wearing a shirt. Or bra. Or pants. Jerking up the bedspread so she could peer underneath, she was relieved to see she at least wore panties.

Did I have sex with Trick?

Panic infused her, but it subsided when memories of the night before returned—with a vengeance. Her getting Trick to move the slave brand's location, then stripping naked, and following him into the bathroom, where she tried to climb all over him...

She thumped the pillow over her head in embarrassment.

I can't believe I did that.

And Trick had been horrified, wrapped in a shower curtain, dripping wet—that was clear as day in her memories, despite how inebriated she had been. *What was in that drink?* It certainly wasn't a regular mead, to get her so drunk.

But the worst part of the whole silly affair?

That Trick had behaved with honor. More honor than Paschar ever had. The one time she had become drunk with her former lover, he had happily taken what was offered, then lectured her the following morning on her lack of decorum and chastity.

She'd never over-imbibed near him again.

I haven't been drunk in over forty years.

She certainly hadn't intended to be last night.

And I have never come on so strong to a male before. I am going to have to apologize.

Shoving the pillow off her face, she opened her eyes to an empty room. *Thank the Lord.*

Sliding out from the sheets, she looked around for her clothes. There, in a pile on her bag. *Trick must have put them there.* Her cheeks warm from embarrassment, she hastily dressed, then went to the bathroom to brush her teeth. By the time she'd emerged, Trick had returned, with a tray of food and what smelled like coffee.

"How's the head?" He placed the tray on the small table.

"Okay." She stepped toward the table, and he slid away, toward the other side of the room. She tracked his movements, her gaze falling on a pillow and folded blanket near the doorway.

He slept on the floor.

After he'd called 'dibs' on the bed.

He didn't even try to share the bed with me.

She scrunched up her nose. She didn't like having to reevaluate her opinion on people, but it appeared that she had been wrong in her earlier thoughts on Trick. He might still be ruthless, and a general annoying ass, but he was also capable of being kind, which was a rare quality in any being.

Living in the Human World has softened you.

"You don't like coffee?" he asked, noting her expression. He dropped his gaze back to his cellphone soon after.

"I like it." She poured herself a cup, and then stared at the food options: scrambled eggs or cereal and toast. She decided on the latter two.

An awkward silence descended on the room, and she took a sip of coffee to delay her humiliation. *Just do it.*

With a sigh, she lowered her cup and sat in the chair. "I am very sorry about last night."

Trick whipped his head up. "What?"

She gritted her teeth. "I am sorry about last night."

He waved a hand in the air. "You drank nearly an entire jug of Djinn spiced mead. That stuff will knock even the sturdiest demon on their ass."

"But my behavior—"

He grinned, exposing brilliant white teeth in an expression that only served to highlight his handsomeness. "Djinn mead is made by adding a single drop of Djinn blood to a barrel. It's highly sought-after and expensive. But because it's mixed with Djinn blood, it severely lowers inhibitions when drunk to excess. One or two glasses, and you would have just had a warm buzz. But three or more?" He chuckled. "I was lucky to escape."

Dismay burned through her. "Are you saying I could have...raped you?" She hid her face in her hands as she thought over the evening again, remembering how she had wrestled him on the bed.

Paschar was right. I need to learn better control.

She'd never thought she would agree with him. It hurt to be proven wrong.

Trick placed a hand on her shoulder; she hadn't even heard him move. "I may not be a trained warrior, but I can hold my own in a fight."

"That doesn't make me feel better." Shame spiraled through her. "What if you hadn't been? What if you weren't as strong as me?"

"You would have stopped if I wasn't interested, of that I have no doubt." He shrugged and stepped away. "Problem was, Trick Junior was more than willing to accommodate you and you knew it. I just figured you'd hate me for it today."

"Trick Junior?"

He winked, earning a surprised laugh from her. *How did he do it?* He'd somehow managed to reassure her, calm her down, and make her laugh, all in the space of five minutes. And she didn't deserve it.

"I really am sorry."

He smirked. "Not as sorry as me for saying no. But alas, missing out is my lot in life."

Seraphina rolled her eyes. "You are so deprived."

He grinned.

She finished her breakfast in silence, but it was a companionable silence. She was strangely at peace just being in the room with Trick. "I think I might have a shower. I smell of sweat and mead."

"Okay, I'll just be checking emails. I've been trying to find out if there's any sign of when Lucifer will open Sheol back up. I definitely won't be picturing you naked and wet." He flashed her a grin. "Oh, did I say that out loud?"

"Jerk."

"You love it." He returned his attention to his phone.

On impulse, she stood and strode over to where he sat in the corner. Leaning down, she kissed his cheek—just a swift press of her lips against his jaw. "Thanks."

Then she hightailed it out of the room, so she couldn't see his expression.

On the other side of the bathroom door, she stood with her back pressed to the timber panel and focused on breathing. She'd just willingly kissed Trick. Sure, it was just a peck, but she'd done it.

And it had felt right, like she could kiss Trick on the cheek like that for the rest of their lives, and it would be the rightest thing in the world.

I think I like him.

Trick had proven he was someone she could trust—he hadn't taken advantage of her, even though he could have. Instead, he'd hobbled around the room wearing a shower curtain while dodging her advances.

If the mead lowers inhibitions, it means that deep down, I want to have sex with Trick.

It was a terrible idea.

But it wasn't as if she had stayed faithful to Paschar's memory—she'd been with other men. And she might be dead in two days' time. She may never know physical passion again.

Why not with Trick?

He would do right by her, she knew. And he could keep it professional afterward, she'd seen the way he handled the members of his guild…

But the most important question: Did she want to do die without ever knowing what it was like to be with him?

CHAPTER 29

Rowan straightened her sky-blue silk shirt and checked to make sure her hair was perfectly slicked back in its bun. There. She was ready.

I can't believe I am doing this.

Climbing out the limousine, she squinted against the bright Miami sunlight. She'd become a tad obsessed with Luke M. Starre's private collection, to the point where she had tracked him down through her colleagues and called him. She'd reached his PA and explained that she was a researcher and would like a better look at some of the items listed in his catalogue.

An hour later, Luke himself had called her back and, after talking with her for a little while, had offered her the chance to view some of the items in person. He'd even sent a private jet to collect her.

This guy has serious money.

Despite it being winter, the air was still sticky with humidity, the piercingly blue sky soaring overhead, cloudless and pristine.

Right now, her home was covered in a fine layer of

snow.

Luke's home—correction, mansion—stretched out before her, three stories high, with white rendering punctuated by navy blue shutters and roof. There were immense double doors at the entry, and a koi pond was located to her left. She'd passed a tennis court on the way up the driveway. *I bet the backyard has a pool. It has to have a pool.*

Even Gran couldn't afford a place like this. And Gran was rich as Hell from owning her hocus-pocus shop.

Don't just stand there.

Gathering her thoughts, she strode toward the huge doors and pressed the doorbell, hearing it chime off in the distance. Thirty seconds passed; a minute. She was at the point of wondering if she should ring the bell again when it was answered.

A young man in his twenties—maybe a year or two younger than her—stood on the other side of the portal. He was incredibly handsome, with features so clean-cut they put statues to shame. In fact, he was even better looking than Seraphina and her colleague, Mr. Trick.

And she hadn't thought that was possible.

He had long brown hair tied up in a bun and a short beard, all so well-groomed it made her painstakingly slicked-back hair look like a bird's nest. His eyes were a gray so pale they almost appeared white, and they contrasted starkly against his blue-framed glasses. He wore a dark gray suit, white shirt, and had a tartan handkerchief tucked in his breast pocket.

He had the hipster vibe down pat, complete with his exposed ankles, and lack of tie.

"Rowan Broome?"

Blinking, she realized she'd just been staring at him. Heat flushed her cheeks. "Yes. I'm looking for Mr. Starre?"

"You're looking right at him."

"Really? I mean, uh, nice to meet you." He was much younger than she had assumed. She held out a hand; he simply looked at it.

She was about to remove it when his arm shot out, and he clasped her palm. But rather than shake it as she had intended, he raised her hand to his lips and pressed a soft kiss to it. *How quaint.*

"Trust me, the pleasure is all mine. Do come in." He released her and stepped back into the entryway.

Rowan followed him inside, her attention snared by the beautiful wooden floors, white walls, and lovely artwork that graced the foyer. "Is that a Rembrandt?"

"It is. You have a discerning eye, I see." He seemed pleased.

"Thank you."

"Now, which pieces in my collection were you interested in seeing?" He slid his hands into his pockets.

"As I said on the phone, my specialty is the Egyptian Old Kingdom." She withdrew the book from her leather satchel. "I noticed you have a statue you claim is a representation of Khufu, the second pharaoh of the Fourth Dynasty, and a sarcophagus you credit to Menes, the first pharaoh of the First Dynasty." While she did hope to see the *Amenonuhoko,* she hadn't been able to pass up the opportunity to view these two items. If real, they were the archaeological finds of the century. There was only one complete three-dimensional statue of Khufu on record, and the remains of Menes — the first ever pharaoh, the one to unite the two Egyptian kingdoms—had *never* been found.

It was almost physically painful that they might have been kept hidden in a private collection for so long.

His gaze locked on the book. "You mentioned a third item?"

"Yes. I have a minor interest in Japanese archaeology, and I saw you had a replica of the *Amenonuhoko*." She'd spent the previous morning perfecting the pronunciation of the word. If she was interested in Japanese culture, then she should be able to speak without her American accent interfering with it. She wanted to appear authentic, like she had no ulterior motive for being here.

"How fortunate. I believe all three items are in the same gallery. Follow me." He walked toward a central staircase that led to a second floor.

She hesitated at the bottom, wondering all of a sudden if this had been a wise idea. She didn't know this man; he might be a rapist or a serial killer luring unsuspecting victims in with his wealth and amazing artifact collection.

He's an art collector. Dr. Phalathropolis vouched for him.

Luke was waiting for her.

Fighting another blush, she hurried to meet him. "Your house is exquisite."

"Thank you." He strode up the stairs quickly, and she grew slightly out of breath trying to keep up.

They reached the first floor, and he turned left. "This way. What got you interested in archaeology?"

"I was always interested in history. It wasn't until I was twelve that I realized you could actually study it for a living."

He shot her a bland glance. "Your parents didn't tell

you sooner?"

"They wanted me to get into the family business. And then they died in a car crash, so they never got the chance to see that I did."

His gray eyes lingered on her face. "I am sorry for your loss. Ah." They entered a bright gallery, with windows angled to maximize the sunlight. "Here we are."

"Don't you have to be careful with the sun exposure?" Some artifacts deteriorated faster when exposed to UV.

"Yes, I have a microfilm laid on the windows to minimize glare, and I also have automatic blinds that descend when a certain lumen level is detected."

She realized she was gaping and shut her mouth with a click. "That is more advanced tech than at most museums."

He gave her a self-depreciating smile. "I have more money than most museums."

The reminder slammed her back to reality. This was a man who had some of the most priceless possessions the world had never seen at his very fingertips. Of course, he could afford to take care of them properly.

They reached the center of the room, and a table with a cloth covering it. Beside it, and similarly swathed, was a sarcophagus.

"Here they are." He whipped the material away from the table, exposing two items to her view.

She whistled.

There, in alabaster, was an Old Kingdom carving of a pharaoh. It wasn't as elaborate in design as the later art from the Middle and New Kingdoms, but it was clearly a representation of the king. "How do you know it is Khufu?"

The statue was of a full body, with Red crown, rounded face and broad chin. He held a flail in his right hand and sat on a throne. It was very similar to the ivory Khufu statuette housed in the Egyptian Museum.

Luke slid on a pair of cotton gloves, then picked the statue up. It was the length of his forearm. He rotated it until she could see the back of the throne—Khufu's name was inscribed in hieroglyphs on the back.

"Oh my god."

This could be the real thing.

Excitement burned through her, making her almost giddy. "Can I touch it?"

"With gloves." He nodded at a smaller pair left on the table.

She quickly put them on and held her hands out for the figurine. It was heavy. Her gaze swept over the stone object with delight. Oh, to be able to study this at length. "Do you have its provenance?"

"The Great Pyramid of Giza."

She almost dropped the statue. Panicking, she shoved it back at Luke. "The pyramid was robbed, probably during the New Kingdom."

He tilted his head, his stare piercing. "I am very careful in tracking the origin of the artifacts I collect."

Rowan wanted to argue that he was wrong—that there was no way this was a real statue of Khufu, and from his tomb, no less. But she didn't want to be rude. And she had the sense that Luke could be dangerous when riled.

He seemed to be waiting for a response.

"When did you buy it?"

"It's been in the family for generations." He carefully

laid it on the table.

"That is amazing. If your sources are correct, then this artifact is priceless." She shot him a narrow glance. "And it should be in a museum where anyone can study it."

He spread his arms wide. "I have opened my collection to you. I am not hiding it."

No, but she knew the Egyptian government would want to get their hands on it, as soon as possible.

Changing the subject, she focused on the *Amenonuhoko*. "The spear is smaller than I anticipated."

Luke titled his head at the artifact. It was about twelve inches long, with tiny inlaid jewels where the blade was hafted to the wooden pole. "Yes, it is quite compacted in this form."

This form?

Was there another replica out there?

"May I?" She indicated the spear with her hand.

"Of course, but don't drop it." A charming smile prevented the reprimand from coming across as harsh. A ringing cell interrupted the moment, and Luke frowned. "Excuse me." He answered the call and strode toward the other end of the gallery.

Fighting another blush—*damn my skin*—she picked up the *Amenonuhoko*. The detail work on it was amazing, and it was heavier in her hands than she would have suspected.

Here it is.

Do I really want to tell Gran's clients about it?

Luke might own artifacts that he shouldn't, but he clearly took excellent care of them. If Seraphina and Mr. Trick stole it, then who was to say they would be care for it any better?

They say they are going to give it back to the rightful owner.

And Seraphina seemed trustworthy. It was like everything she said was backed by truth.

Luke returned. "I am so sorry, but I must leave in a few minutes."

Disappointment crashed through her. "That's okay."

"First, feel free to take any photographs you need. And here." He swept the material away from the sarcophagus. "You may study this first."

Her eyes bulged at the beautiful stonework. Its paint was still intact, and the design was simple. Nothing like the elaborate decorations of the later-dynasty pharaohs, but that was insignificant. In the center of the sarcophagus was the cartouche for Menes.

Her fingers clenched into fists.

Holy. Shit.

"Was it empty when you found it?" She ran a gloved hand wonderingly over the sarcophagus.

"No, there is a mummy inside."

"You mean 'was'?"

"No, I mean *is*. I never—I mean, it was never removed."

"Oh my god." If she could get access to the remains and have them DNA tested... "This is amazing."

Satisfaction gleamed in his pale eyes. "I am glad you approve."

"Thank you for showing me these."

"You are *most* welcome. Now, I apologize, but I have other business I must attend to."

"Of course."

Luke led her out the gallery, and back down the staircase to the front door. She thanked him again, and then hurried to the waiting limousine. He had insisted she fly back to New York in his jet.

Settling into the car, she chewed on a fingernail as she debated whether or not to tell her grandmother about the visit.

I should call Eric. Tell him about the find. He was an art historian—he'd be equally excited.

But she owed her Gran so much.

Pulling out her phone, she texted, I KNOW WHERE IT IS.

CHAPTER 30

"So, is the feather yours?" Trick asked. He was responding to an avalanche of emails as Seraphina did yoga on the floor of their room.

The angel paused in the warrior pose and tilted her head to the side. "The black one?"

"No. Although, I was going to ask you about that, too." He nodded his head in her direction. "The one on your necklace."

Her gaze dropped to the floor. "You saw that."

Shame, he realized. She was ashamed.

"Is it yours?"

"Yes."

"I'm surprised they let you keep it."

"They don't know I took it."

"Good on you." Trick nodded his approval, pride at her actions swelling within his chest. When an angel lost their wings, they lost *all* of their wings—you were left no mementos. To be exiled and manage to sneak away a piece of your former self while it happened?

Seraphina 1, Archangels 0.

"I shouldn't have kept it," she said, sliding sinuously into another yoga pose.

"They were your wings."

"But I lost them."

"On a trumped-up charge. I told Uriel as much."

She lost her balance and toppled over. "You chastised *Uriel*?"

"Yup, and I'd do it again." He shut his tablet off. No more emails; his brain would melt out of his ears. And if he had to reply to another request from Orphi about that damned larval cat...

How much were they? He turned the tablet back on.

"But he's an archangel."

"Sure is. But he's also an ass."

She gasped. "Trick!"

Five thousand dollars?

That's how much one of those cats cost?

And Metcalf ate the damned thing?

No wonder the assassin was pissed. But not angry enough to take on the Reynard's Imp personally.

"Uriel is powerful. He's—"

"An ass." Trick looked up, shoving thoughts of larval cats to the side. "I don't answer to him, and they made you a scapegoat. He knows it, I know it. Hell, half of Hell knows it. One day you'll get your wings back, and you'll know not to trust him."

Her voice was small, stripped of its usual confidence. "But he's an archangel."

"Yes." Trick leaned forward. "But that doesn't make him right, or good. He was chosen to lead, and lead he shall, but that doesn't mean he was picked because of his virtue."

She frowned. "You sound passionate about it."

He shrugged. "I don't like it when people get put on pedestals. It's a long way for them to fall. And you don't want to be the one crushed when they do."

"That's a harsh view."

"Life is harsh."

"True."

"So, you going to tell me about the black feather?" He pushed the tablet to the side, his undivided attention on her.

"It's none of your business."

"You're my slave, it's my business."

Something like hurt flashed in her eyes at the mention of her slavery, and it made him wince. But facts were facts, and if she was clandestinely chasing after some black-winged angel, then it could spell trouble for the guild.

And he wouldn't tolerate anything that disrupted his guild, even for her.

What do you mean, even for her?

He didn't want to delve too deeply into that thought. But he knew he cared about her, more than he should. Sure, he lusted after her, but he admired her, too. Her poise, her slight acts of rebellion, her calm. And most of all, her heart. She'd given up her freedom for another.

Trick knew firsthand there weren't many people who would be willing to do the same.

"So, who do you think this feather belongs to?" Trick asked, when she stayed quiet.

"I don't know for sure, but I was hoping it belonged to an angel called Dina. You may have heard of her."

Dina.

"I've come across her name before." She was on the cusp of ascending to archangel status, so the rumors went. And she'd been a power to be reckoned with for centuries. She'd had the respect of other angels, and the fear of demons. She was known as the beautiful death.

Seraphina gave him a slanted look. "See, that was the truth. But whenever you speak, it is always layered, like there's a lie there I can't pinpoint."

"I always tell the truth."

A smile bloomed, one that made her eyes twinkle. She looked breathtaking. "Now, I know you are lying."

"Caught me. Now, why do you think it's this Dina's feather?"

"She was our captain. She was kidnapped by the same Infernus demons who took Z. We haven't heard of her since then."

An angel that powerful was kidnapped? By *Infernus*? It was hard to credit. Z? Yes, sure; despite being strong for his years he wasn't that old. But Dina?

"But why do you think she'd have black wings?" He'd never heard of such a thing.

"I don't know. She was taken, we haven't heard from her, but suddenly, there's rumors of an angel with black wings. Maybe she's been dyeing them?"

Doubtful, but he didn't want to crush the hope in her eyes. This black-winged angel could just be a demon using a powerful glamor spell, or a fallen angel who'd somehow managed to regain their feathers.

"You want to find the feather's owner," he said.

"I think Lamar knows something."

"He won't say anything." When you ran a tavern that specialized in information, you had to be careful about who you gave that intel to. If the black-winged angel was Dina, the Djinn wouldn't be stupid enough to tell anyone her identity, unless she'd given the okay.

Lamar had strong survival instincts.

"I could—"

Trick strode over to her and placed his hands on her shoulders. "Do *not* try and 'convince' Lamar to tell you anything."

Her eyes flashed. "You just don't want me to mess things up for the guild."

"There is that," he allowed. "But Lamar is stronger than you'd think. And he has immense reach throughout all three Hell-realms. You mess with him, and you place a target on your back. You'll be dead in a week."

"If we don't die in two days."

He nodded. "I'm not saying give up, but be careful." He gave her shoulders a final squeeze and let go.

Her hand shot out, and she grabbed his wrist. "Why do you care? Worried you'll lose your asset?"

He turned his forearm, seizing her arm in return. "I don't want you to die."

Her mouth opened in shock as she perceived the truth of his statement. "You mean that."

"I do."

Her eyes went wide, and a moment later, she pressed her mouth to his, the kiss gentle and sweet.

He pulled away and looked around the room. "I told Lamar not to give you any more mead!"

She laughed, the sound pealing and wonderful.

CHAPTER 31

Seraphina stepped closer, until barely a hair's breadth separated them. His heat pressed against her, her skin hyperaware of his proximity. Her nipples puckered, and the blood pooled low in her belly.

Trick's face was so impossibly handsome.

Lust like she had never known pulsed through her. It made her drunken approaches last night seem foolish and hasty. Why would she want to rush this?

"Are you sure you've not had any mead?" Trick raised an eyebrow.

"None."

"Then why are you—?"

She pressed her chest to his. "Because I want to."

"You must still be drunk," he muttered.

"I am frighteningly sober."

She may only have two days left to live. Dina might have black wings. They only had one piece of the Heart. And it seemed like Seraphina would never see Heaven again.

If these are my last days, I want to enjoy them.

Having sex with Trick would be very, very enjoyable.

"I am not sure this is a good idea." He stepped back, holding up his hands in protest.

"I think it's a great idea."

"That's the boredom talking."

"You're saying you don't want to sleep with me?"

"Oh, honey. I don't want to *sleep* with you. I want to fuck you silly. But I don't think this is a good idea."

"It's a great idea." She ran a palm down his chest.

He groaned. "I'm your slave master."

"Not for long."

He *tsked*. "You owe me ten million dollars."

"I am efficient."

He chuckled, and she could see his determination wavering.

"It's your choice." Reluctantly, she dropped her hand.

Trick's pupils expanded as he stared at her. He muttered something like "God help me" and then his mouth crashed against hers, his arms wrapping around her waist, tugging her close.

Yes.

His tongue entangled with hers, his taste reminding her of sky lilies, a delicacy she'd once had in Heaven. Hungry for more, Seraphina slid her arms around his neck, pressing her chest against the hard planes of his torso. His heart pounded against hers, and the two beats synchronized as passion flowed between them. Tingles swept through her entire body, centering on her belly, on her core. She ran her hands over his shoulder-blades, before dipping them down to tug his shirt from his trousers.

Trick pulled away for a moment, and she almost

keened at the loss. He jerked his shirt over his head, before pressing a hot kiss to her jaw, then down the column of her neck. His hands swept over her torso and along the underside of her breasts, making her body ache for more.

For *him*.

Leaning back, she tugged her own shirt off, then her bra. *There*. Skin to skin. His rock-hard abs formed a silken wall against her torso, while her breasts rubbed against his pecs. Her blood pumped through her, hot and languid.

"You taste amazing," Trick muttered, his mouth moving with agonizing slowness down her chest, reaching the top of her right breast.

"So, do you."

Finally, his mouth settled over the mound of her breast, before dipping down lower, to her aching nipple. Her fingers clawed through his hair, pinning him to the spot. He growled in approval.

Trick's hand slid past the waistband of her trousers as he kissed her, tension building within her, stronger than any lust she'd known previously. Her trousers disappeared and she was left naked, but for her feather.

This time it was natural, normal, like this should have happened before, and would happen again.

His fingers traced gently over her lower stomach, before sliding along the lips of her sex. A moment later, they dipped within.

"You're so wet."

His growled words made her arousal soar, and she moved against his clever fingers, working her body against his hand until pleasure exploded within her. Her mouth open in a silent scream, she shuddered through the drugging ecstasy that spread through her every limb.

"Fuck, you're responsive." Trick was on his feet again, and then they were kissing, the passion between them rising to blistering levels. She reached between them, grabbing his hard length in one hand, stroking over the velvet-coated steel.

"You feel amazing," she murmured against his mouth.

And he would feel even better inside her.

Hooking a leg over his hips, she angled her body until he was pressed against her core. Trick stroked his length over her, up and down, making her want to scream. Then he slid within her, stretching her, becoming one with her.

She came again.

Trick swallowed her scream, began to move quickly, faster, harder, as their tongues danced to an age-old rhythm. Pleasure overloaded her senses, and she angled her hips, meeting him thrust for thrust. Trick became the center of her focus; every movement, every breath only served to heighten their pleasure.

Trick's head fell back and his eyes shut, a low groan filling the air as he reached his climax. The feel of him within her made the pleasure spiral out of control, and she came, squeezing about him so hard he cursed his way through a second orgasm.

When it was over, they stood wrapped about each other, her head on his shoulder.

Sex had never been that good before, and they hadn't even made it to a bed.

Trick picked her up in a smooth lift, then deposited her on the mattress. He joined her there, lying on his back, breathing hard.

"That was—"

"Amazing."

"We should do it again," Trick said. "But in another ten minutes or so."

She laughed.

Joy, she realized. *He gives me joy.*

"While we're waiting, why don't you tell me about yourself."

Trick turned his face to look at her. "There's not much to know."

"Humor me."

"All right. But only because you just gave me two mind-blowing orgasms." He raised his arms, resting his head on his hands. "I was the middle child. I have an older sister, and a younger brother. My sister was perfect, powerful and disdainful. My parents had decided to pair for my birth, so that they would get the optimum offspring. Instead, they got me." He flashed her a look, which she met. "When I failed to rise to the appropriate level of power, my father left, and my mother married, having another son. He wasn't powerful, but he hadn't been bred to become the ultimate weapon, either."

Bred to become a weapon? What kind of demon was he?

"My brother was unbalanced. My mother said he was just spirited, emotional, and that he'd mature with age. But I knew better. I watched him. And then one day, I found he'd captured and tortured a demon, keeping this female as a sex slave. In his little hideaway, I found the bones of many others. This wasn't the first time he'd done it."

She bit her lip. "Do many demons care about these

things?"

"No, but I did."

Truth.

"And so I helped the demon girl. I got her free, got her to safety, and then my brother told my parents. They believed him, and they disowned me."

Truth.

"What about your sister?"

"Neemah has always been too quick to judge. She believed what my brother and mother said, never asked me."

"And so you set up your own mercenary guild."

"And so I did."

"I bet they regret their actions now."

Bitterness swept through his brown eyes. "I doubt it. Money and my kind of power don't mean much to them."

"What happened to the girl?"

"She joined the guild for a while. She left a few centuries ago to pursue her own interests. She has a thing for vigilante justice."

Sadness for Trick's past made her throat ache, but apart from the slight moment of bitterness, he hadn't seemed too upset by it.

"What about you?" he asked.

"I was an only child. My mother and father doted on me. I thought I was in love, just before I fell. I even got engaged on the day."

His mouth thinned. "But the fucker left you when he found out you fell, didn't he?"

She nodded, but there was no pain with the thought. Just anger.

"The part that upsets me the most? I didn't get to say

goodbye to my family. To explain what happened. And that I didn't wise up to my former lover's nature before now."

"Ah, we were both played."

Peace settled over her. *We were.* But she wouldn't be a fool again.

On impulse, she tugged the feather over her head. "Here."

"What are you doing?"

"Giving it to you."

"Why?"

"Because everyone deserves something given freely to them, at least once in their life. This is my gift to you."

He took it with something almost like reverence in his expression. He tugged the chain over his head and patted it when the feather settled over his heart. "Thank you."

Rolling onto her side, she gave him a saucy grin. "Now, what can you give me?"

"How about I surprise you?"

"Mmm, I do like surprises."

CHAPTER 32

Sheol's barriers had dropped. They could leave.

Trick stared at his phone for a few moments, then looked at Seraphina. She slept, one arm over her eyes, sheltering them from the burgeoning daylight.

Last night—all of yesterday, really—had been amazing. Better than amazing. He still couldn't feel his toes, or his balls. But it had been worth it. He's never had a sexual partner who fit him so well.

I could spend the next decade with her, and it wouldn't be enough.

But even if Hades didn't kill them in the next few hours, she was going to leave the guild as soon as she could. And he didn't blame her. He'd do the same.

He played with the feather around his neck. He shouldn't have taken it, but she'd offered, and the tiny piece of Heaven against his heart was welcome.

He placed a gentle hand on her bicep. "Time to wake up, princess. It's our last day."

Seraphina's arm moved to the side whip-fast, and she had a hand around his throat before he could blink. He held still, not wanting to trigger any other lethal reflexes.

She was a warrior before she fell. Idiot.

He just hadn't realized her reflexes were that fast, even for an angel. He wasn't entirely sure he could take her in a fight.

Awareness crept into her eyes, and she let him go with a jerk. "I'm so sorry."

"No harm done." He fought the urge to rub his abused trachea.

She clenched her fists. "I left a mark."

"It will heal. Anyway, it doesn't matter. The barrier around Sheol is down. We can leave."

Excitement gleamed in her eyes, before they turned dull. Was she disappointed their stolen interlude was about to end?

Probably not.

She only viewed him as a temporary situation, anyway.

"We don't have time to search both his houses," she said. "What if we're wrong? What if it isn't even in the Human Realm? We only have one day left."

One day.

He'd fought for every day of his existence for the past thousand years. He wasn't about to give up now.

"We ask for an extension." He doubted Hades would grant it, but there *had* been extenuating circumstances.

"I'll get dressed." Seraphina reached for her phone, skimming the messages waiting for her.

She froze. "Oh, my Lord."

"What? What is it?" He tried to read over her shoulder, then recalled that he'd told her off for doing the same thing previously.

"Rowan's found it."

"Who?"

"Dora's granddaughter. She found the spear."

"*How*?"

Seraphina stared at her cellphone, horrified. "She went to Lucifer's in person. Dora is going to kill us."

"What? Who cares about Dora? Rowan will have given us away! Now Lucifer *and* Hades will want us dead."

"She told him she was a researcher." She lowered her arm. "Trick, she doesn't believe in magic. And she met Lucifer himself."

"Fuck." He shoved a hand through his hair. "But you know what this means?"

She met his gaze. "We might live to see tomorrow."

He grinned. "We might indeed. But first, I need to see Hades."

"You fucked up, Trick." Hades' glower would have made a more sensible man tremble. Trick just shrugged.

"You're asking us to steal from *Lucifer*. The job has inherently more risks." Trick sat down on the rickety chair opposite Hades' desk. The god's office was as cluttered as Trick's was fastidiously neat, crammed floor to ceiling with books, and with a gargoyle statue shoved in one corner. Someone had put a party hat on its head.

The god crossed his arms over his massive chest. "You only have one day left. I'd be out looking for the spear, rather than wasting time here."

"About that..."

"I am not giving you an extension. The deadline is tonight, midnight. Or you're dead." Something like regret glittered in the god's yellow gaze, before quickly vanishing.

It was probably a good thing Trick had left Seraphina back at the guild. She wouldn't be impressed with their unchanged deadline. As it was, she'd spluttered with annoyance that she'd been left behind. He'd told her to track Sylvester down and get as many breaking-and-entering spells as possible.

Trick leaned forward. "We know where the spear is."

"You do?" Both of Hades' eyebrows rose.

"I just need a small favor."

"What kind of favor?" The eyebrows arched down again into a frown.

"A metallurgical kind."

"Hrm." The god rubbed his chin. "I may know a guy for that."

Trick smiled, smug. "Thought you might."

Now, he just needed to call in another favor.

Trick teleported Seraphina and himself into the alley behind the Cat on a Broomstick. It was deserted and smelled of old vomit and urine. *Wonderful.* And Peony had said Tartarus stank.

They only had an hour. They had to make it to Lucifer's house and daylight was wasting.

Hurrying around to the front entrance, they were greeted by a glaring Dora Broome. "You dare show your face here?"

Seraphina held up her hands. "What did we do?"

The Crone wagged a finger. "Do you *know* who my granddaughter went and introduced herself to?"

"We didn't tell her to do that. We *never* would have suggested it," Trick replied. It exposed *them* to too much risk. Especially since the girl didn't believe in magic.

"Hmph." Dora turned on her heel and marched along the rambling pathway through the shop.

They followed her to the small room at the back of the store, where Trick sat on the sofa, Seraphina next to him. Dora paced the room. "She has met *Lucifer*. He invited her back to view his collection again. He flew her to Miami in his *private jet*."

"Why didn't you stop her?" Trick asked.

Dora whirled on him. "Me? She didn't even tell me!"

"You're going to have to wipe her memory." The deep voice made the Crone start, and they all turned to see Hades, who had suddenly appeared in the room.

Dora eyed the god like he was a piece of candy, then scowled. "What is a god doing here?"

"This isn't just any god," Trick said. "It's Hades."

Dora glared at the god. "So what does he want? I'm not dead yet."

"Bring the girl here." Hades waved a hand.

Dora's mouth set in a thin line. "I don't have to do anything you say."

"You're not dead yet, but you will be one day. You might regret not assisting me now."

"Are you threatening my *soul*?"

Hades grinned. "Yes."

The witch murmured a number of unflattering comments, but plucked out her cell. A few minutes later, the young redheaded woman entered the room. Her eyes nearly bulged out of her face when she spotted Hades.

He was rather spectacular looking, especially for humans.

Rowan met the Crone's gaze. "Gran?"

Dora nodded. "Do what this gentleman says."

Hades pulled out a metal rod and handed it to the girl. "Take a seat, then hold this, and picture the *Amenonuhoko* very clearly in your mind. The look of it, the feel, the weight."

"Why would I do that?"

"Because I asked you to."

Rowan took the rod reluctantly and sat down on a chair. "I really don't see what this will achieve."

Dora turned to her grandchild. "Please, Rowan. Do what he says."

With a sigh, the redhead closed her eyes and concentrated. As she did, the rod changed, morphing in her hands. By the time she opened her eyes, an exact replica of the *Amenonuhoko* lay in her palms.

Seems a bit small. Had she remembered it correctly?

"What the—?" Shock suffused her face.

"Thank you." Hades snatched it from her.

"I don't understand." Rowan turned to her gran beseechingly.

"I'm going to wipe her memories now." Hades played with the miniature spear.

"Wipe my—you can't do that!" Rowan jumped to her feet. A second later, she thumped back into her chair, rage and confusion warring on her face. "What's happening? Why can't I move?"

"Poorly done, Theodora, keeping your kin ignorant."

Dora glared. "It wasn't my choice. And it's rude of you to tie her up."

"Ignorant of what?" Rowan cried, struggling against her invisible bonds.

Hades squatted down in front of her. "Magic."

She laughed. "There is no such thing."

The god sighed. "Such a stubborn mind." He twisted the spear in his hands. "Which memories should I leave?"

"Just take out Seraphina and Trick," Dora said, mouth set in an angry line. "Leave anything to do with the *Amenonuhoko* as if it was her own idea."

Wild green eyes sought out Dora. "Gran! You can't allow them to do this. I'm not a lab rat. You can't do this to me!"

"This is beyond my choice. You got in over your head." Dora looked sad, but resolute.

"I just looked at some artifacts!"

"If only it were that simple," Hades said, reaching for the girl's head. He glanced over at Trick, then handed him the spear. "You get moving, I will clean up this mess."

"Mess? What mess?" Rowan demanded, still struggling, dodging the god's palm.

As Trick teleported them out, he felt a moment of pity for the human girl. Life had a way of shitting on people, and she'd just learned that the hard way.

CHAPTER 33

They were inside Lucifer's Miami home. It had taken a battery of spells that Seraphina had 'liberated' from Sylvester—she'd beaten him in an arm-wrestling match, to the delight of the guild members present—and a few acrobatics, but they were in.

It was a spectacular mansion, light and airy, and put Raze's palatial dwelling to shame. Seraphina didn't want to stare, but she found it hard to keep her eyes from the priceless artworks and artifacts.

They still hadn't found the spear.

"According to my sources, Lucifer is back at the Tower of Tortures." Trick's voice was soft against her ear.

"So, let's keep hunting." The sun was already beginning to set. They only had a few hours left before their deadline.

Invisible, they swept through the mansion, careful to keep out of the way of the demon staff. Trick was constantly talking to Sylvester through an ear-piece. The other demon wasn't with them, but had decided to watch the action 'live'. He was giving Trick updates on the technological defenses and how to get past them.

Seraphina was coming to realize that the two demons were friends, and Sylvester was the best thief she'd ever encountered.

He should be doing this. He wouldn't screw it up.

They had reached the third and top floor of the mansion before they found it. It was...small. Only about a foot long, it rested on a stand in a glass case. Rowan had been right in her recollection of the artifact's dimensions.

Now I know how humans feel when they view the Mona Lisa.

It was amazing, but it was also a little bit of a letdown.

Carefully, they crept toward the glass cabinet. It was in the middle of the room, in a line of display cases marching toward the end of the gallery. *Lucifer's house is like a museum.* More space was dedicated to displaying his ornate collection than for living purposes.

Trick leaned over to her. "Sylvester says there are likely to be pressure sensors near the cabinet."

They studied the spear in its protective casing. It glittered with magical spells, most written in angelic.

"How many alarms do you think we'll set off?"

"Too many," Trick replied. He glanced around the room.

"Give me the fake." She held out her hand.

Trick stared at it for a moment. "Not just yet. I want a closer look."

She clenched her fist. "We need to be quick."

"We will be."

They approached the cabinet, Trick holding the bogus spear Hades had created close to his torso. He dropped a neon-glowing crystal on the floor, stepped over it, then drew a series of counter-spells on the glass. Finally, he threw a bag of powder on the cabinet, which dissolved. "There."

He had the spear in his hand when dust was thrown in her face.

Coughing, Seraphina looked around wildly, instinctively filling her hands with knives.

Power slammed into her, shoving her to the ground. Her knees slammed into the floorboards. She gritted her teeth and fought against it the force, but she was trapped.

"Thief!" The word was snarled.

Lucifer.

He stood ten feet away, his brown hair loose around a face so exquisite it put even the archangel Aurora to shame.

A dagger launched through the air toward her. She struggled against the invisible bonds, but it was hopeless.

I am going to die.

"No!" Trick's shout made her fight harder.

The knife slammed home and she was thrown to the side.

What?

Where?

No pain...

Trick collapsed next to her, the dagger protruding obscenely from his chest. His hand clenched over the hilt.

"*Trick!*"

She was released from her magical bonds and darted forward, cupping his head. Her hands fluttered over his wound, as she tried to work out what to do to save him.

It looked like a heart strike.

Throat clogged, she demanded, "Trick. Why?"

Blood seeped from his lips, and he grinned weakly at her. "Only get...stabbed...by me."

Blood was pooling, sticky, around the dagger. It was a Cushiel—an angel-killer—and deadly to the majority of demon species.

Tears trickled down her cheeks. "No. No, no, *no*."

"Barely hurts." He coughed, and blood sprayed the air.

She lowered her forehead to his. "You're dying."

He met her gaze with his. "Worth it."

"No, I'm not."

He touched her cheek. "So beautiful."

"Teleport out of here. Get help." But his face was growing pale, dark blood bubbling between his lips.

She ripped a healing spell from her pack and poured the liquid directly on the wound. Trick's back arched, and a scream tore through the room. If anything, he looked *worse*.

There is no cure for a Cushiel.

No, she wouldn't accept that.

He had to get better.

He would.

Trick reached out, clasping her wrist in a weak grip. "Get. Away. Save. Self." A moment later, his hand dropped to the ground as he exhaled, the sound rattling deep in his lungs.

Then he was still.

Her fingers scrabbled at his neck, but there was nothing. No pulse.

He was gone.

"*No!*" The scream tore from her. She ripped the dagger from his chest, and pressed down desperately on the wound, willing it to heal.

It didn't work. He didn't move.

The bright vitality that embodied Trick had gone.

"*Trick!*" The scream came from the earpiece.

If I press harder —

"How touching." Lucifer clapped.

Her head whipped up to stare at the first of the fallen.

"Your lover boy is dead. No one steals from me." Lucifer grinned, revealing fangs. His almost-white irises glowed. "You're next."

Tears ran down her cheeks. A ripping, searing pain like she'd never experienced clawed through her. Worse than losing her wings. Worse than Paschar's betrayal.

Trick had given his life for her.

Her.

No one she knew would have done that. Not even her parents.

She looked down at Trick. *I could have loved him.*

Skies, she *had* loved him. At least a little bit.

And that little spark would have grown, would have flourished.

With a raw scream, she threw herself over his body, and slammed into Lucifer. Blades out, she dug them into his belly, over and over.

He fought her, fast and furious, but rage like she had never known suffused her, making her stronger, faster than ever.

With a furious kick, she sent him flying through the glass wall. In a shower of shards, Lucifer hit the ground below, his skull cracking in a bloody spray on the mosaic tiles.

She jumped out after him.

They fought, her cheekbone shattering from his blow, his arm snapping in two from hers. She slammed her blade home in his blackened heart, and it paralyzed him for a bare second. It was all she needed.

Anger fueling her, she sawed through his neck with her other knife. Blood sprayed her in the face, the eyes, her mouth, and it dropped from her hair. Seraphina just bared her teeth and kept cutting through muscle, through tendon, and through the beginning of bone.

Lucifer's hands clawed at her, leaving deep gashes down her arms.

She was almost through his vertebrae when he vanished.

"*No!*" she yelled, the sound raw and primal.

Spinning around, she searched for him, only to draw up short.

Lucifer hadn't vanished. *She had.*

She was in a square room, the walls painted a dull gray, the floor even duller, although the ceiling was white. Fluorescent light spread unevenly over the room, and there was no furniture.

In one corner, stood a shadowed man. Hope surged within her, until she realized he was taller than Trick, stockier.

Trick is dead.

Fury rose in her. "Where am I?"

The man strode into the light.

Laird. Baal. Lucifer's Great Duke.

"You betrayed us!" She launched herself at him, only to be grabbed from behind.

"No, he retrieved you." The person holding her was shaking her. "He teleported you out of there!"

She glared over her shoulder, and some of the fight bled from her. "Sylvester?"

"The one and only." His blue eyes were dull, his face worn.

"Where's Trick? Where's Lucifer? Where am I?" She broke from his hold.

"Trick was gone when I got there. I left Lucifer where he was. You're in my panic room," Laird answered.

Seraphina stalked toward him. "Trick was *gone*? Where?"

"I don't know," Baal replied.

She threw her dagger so hard it embedded in the concrete wall. "I need to find him."

"He's dead. We saw him die." Sylvester's voice turned gravelly. "I felt it."

Laird placed his hands on her shoulders. "You need to calm down, you need to think."

"You stopped me from killing Lucifer!" Faster than a blink, she was behind the god.

Sylvester stepped toward her. "Woah! Did you just teleport?"

"What? No. I can't."

"I think you just did."

Sylvester and Laird glanced meaningfully at each other. Laird cleared his throat. "Do you feel stronger? Faster? More powerful?"

"What I feel is *anger*."

Trick had given his life for her. It was the *least* of the emotions she felt.

"Try to teleport," Laird said.

"Where?"

"Anywhere." He paused. "Wait. Hold my hand when

you do it."

A calloused palm closed around her blood-soaked wrist. She focused on the first place she could think of.

A heartbeat...and Seraphina and Laird were standing on Raze's manicured lawn, the great columned entry of his mansion before them.

"Nice place," the god said.

She turned to him. "I need to find Trick."

"Finding people is difficult. People, they change from day to day, minute to minute. Unless you know everything about them, it can be hard to teleport directly to them."

"So I'll find a way to locate him first."

"Not without a token, you won't."

"A what?"

"If Trick is carrying a static object, something that won't change, that you know inside and out, then you'll be able to find him. That's why teleport-capable demons give each other jewelry when they bond or mate."

"Like an anchor?"

"Yes."

Trick had her feather.

"I can trace him." She met Laird's eyes, radiating pure determination. "I am going after his body, no matter what. He deserves a proper burial."

And who knew, she might be able to bring him back from the grave.

I am not worth dying for.

"Well then, by all means, let me tag along for the ride."

They vanished.

CHAPTER 34

Seraphina!

Was she okay? Had she survived?

Wait. He was dead.

Then why do I hurt? Trick's body was one giant bruise. His back ached most of all.

But didn't he get stabbed in the heart?

And here I thought death was meant to be peaceful.

He sat up and opened his eyes. He was surrounded by white, fluffy and soft mist, like he was inside a cloud. Wisps of air floated around his legs and feet, but it didn't feel like anything. It wasn't even cool.

Am I in Heaven?

He hoped Seraphina had escaped, that he'd bought her enough time to flee Lucifer.

"You." The word was spat out like a curse.

Uriel was to his left, the angel's jet-black skin glinting in the soft sunlight. Michael stood by his side, his white eyes cold and hard, a sword in his hand. Heaven's enforcer.

This isn't good.

When Trick died, he always figured his soul would stop by Hades on its way out the door.

"You couldn't have stayed where you were. Down with all the other rejects in Hell. You had to come back." Uriel snarled the words, his face contorted with rage and disgust.

Come back?

He turned to look over his shoulder, saw a fall of white interwoven with rose-gold filaments.

My wings. They're back.

Power flooded him, healing his wounds, his aches.

My abilities. Before he'd fallen, Trick had been a healer.

Raising a shaking hand to touch the softness, he startled at the sensations that burned through him. Trick had never thought to see his wings again—Hell, he'd written off *ever* returning to Heaven. It's why he'd drunk Hades' blood, why he'd become one of the few true fallen angels out there. Why he'd started the guild, started a new life. Hidden his true nature among a host of demons, so that only Hades, Lucifer and Satan knew his true identity in the Hell-realms.

Seraphina might think she's fallen, but until she drinks the blood of a death god—or Lucifer— she's merely a wingless angel.

Wasn't it hilarious that the archangels never bothered to clarify that distinction?

Fuck, how he hated the assholes.

Trick struggled to his feet, his balance thrown off by wings he hadn't had in over a millennium.

"I will cut them off now. Save having to do it later." Michael stepped forward.

"Leave him alone!" From out of nowhere, Seraphina

darted between Trick and the archangels, her face, hands, and hair splattered in blood.

She was utterly magnificent.

Chin raised, eyes flashing fire, she made his blood pound, and his newly repaired heart race.

"*Seraphina*?" Uriel's gaze widened. "What are you doing here? Leave at once!"

"Don't you touch him." Then she screamed mentally, the word indecipherable, but deafening his mind nonetheless.

The two archangels flinched.

She just threw herself in front of two archangels for me.

Archangels he knew she feared.

I think I love her.

He'd made her his heir, knowing it would boost her abilities if he died, but he was in awe of how strong she had become. *To make archangels wince...*

Uriel raised a hand, as if to strike Seraphina, but froze, his arm suspended in midair.

"I wouldn't do that if I were you."

Baal.

The god must have teleported with Seraphina, his power a golden inferno around him.

A former deposed god, in Heaven.

Oh, how the other angels would scream at the blasphemy.

Trick grinned.

But Baal wasn't the last entity to put in an appearance. The archangel Gabriel arrived in a burst of power, dark hair hanging low over his forehead, his eyes a brilliant violet, wings threaded with thick veins of gold.

To see Gabriel was rare; as Heaven's spymaster, he

tended to keep under the radar.

"Seraphina," he said.

The archangel's eyes took in the fallen angel, something almost tender gracing his expression, before his gaze hardened when he spotted Trick.

"What is going on here?" Gabriel turned to Michael and Uriel. "Why do you have a sword out?"

Michael's eyes flashed. "Precaution."

"He was going to cut my new wings off," Trick offered.

Michael growled.

Seraphina spun around, and her eyes went wide, her expression stunned as she took in his wings. "You're an *angel*?"

"I was. Am."

She touched his wing with a bloody hand, gasping as she stained his new feathers. "Who were you?"

A moment later, the cloud shook, and another archangel appeared.

Great, why don't we call it a party?

This newcomer was female, with hair a deep russet red, and eyes of dark brown. She was barely five feet tall, but her face was a female version of his own. Her voice was clipped and precise. "He was Cassiel."

Nanael. His sister. He'd always called her Neemah; she had enjoyed it when he was a child, tolerated it when he was an adult.

Surprise and grief crossed Seraphina's fine features at the revelation of his name.

Uriel spat. "The healer angel who helped *demons*."

"You dare greet his return with *swords*?" Neemah demanded. "And why was I told of this event by *Gabriel*?

Not by the two angels who met his arrival?"

"It is not your concern, Nanael," Michael said, his grip tightening on his sword.

Neemah stomped her foot. "He is my *brother*."

Trick's legs wobbled, and he sank to the ground.

Seraphina collapsed next to him and he drew his wings around them both. And in doing so, he saw them, the flecks of yellow gold that had appeared in his feathers months before his fall.

Seraphina stared at them too, then at him. "You were about to *ascend*?"

He nodded, pressing his cheek to her blood-splattered hair. "Funny, how when Uriel found out I was going to be an archangel, I got my wings removed and was kicked out of Heaven. And that my side of the story was never heard."

"Lies!" Uriel shouted.

Neemah stepped forward, her white gown flowing around her. "Is this true?"

Trick peeled his left wing away, revealed it to her. "They are exactly as they were the day before I fell."

His sister ran a gentle finger over the fine gold filaments, then whirled to face Uriel. "You dared to cut the wings off an ascending angel?"

"He helped demons!"

"Where was your proof? You never revealed your source!" Neemah raged. "You barred me from the trial."

"My brother," Trick murmured. "My brother was the source."

Seraphina's hand went to her throat.

"Why would he lie? What had he to gain?" Michael asked.

A bell chimed, then Hades' voice drawled, "What indeed?"

Trick turned at the sound of the god's voice. There, in jeans, a black T-shirt, and a black leather jacket stood the god. His hair was out, and his lemon-colored eyes flashed. He bumped fists with Baal.

Two gods, and four archangels.

And one rebirth.

This was the stuff of legends.

Funny, how the only thing I care about is not being dead. And Seraphina being alive.

"This is not your realm," Michael snapped. "You are not welcome here."

"Strange. Uriel doesn't seem to pay attention to that rule," Hades rumbled.

"Uriel?" Neemah turned to the other archangel.

"It was nothing." Uriel slashed his hand through the air.

"Your recent visit to my realm may have been pointless," Hades said, "but still more lacking was your interview with Trick's brother. Perhaps he can fill us in on some of the details you overlooked last time you talked to him." The god clicked his fingers and suddenly Paschar was there, in the clouds with them.

The sniveling bastard.

At first, he didn't see Trick or Seraphina. Instead, he preened in front of the four archangels. Trick came to his feet slowly, sweeping his wings behind his back.

"My lords, how may I be of service?" Paschar bowed low.

Michael stared at Hades. "You *dare* summon an angel?"

Trick's brother turned and went pale at the sight of the Hell-lord. He pivoted back to the archangels. "My lords?"

Uriel rolled his eyes. "Repeat your testimony, Paschar. Did you find your brother healing a demon?"

"What is this about?" Paschar asked, confused. "Cassiel is already fallen."

"Not anymore," Hades grunted.

Paschar spun around, his face morphing into an expression of rage when he spotted Trick. He barely even noticed Seraphina. "What is *he* doing here? And with wings?"

"He won them back."

"I thought you said he wouldn't be given a way back in." Paschar's tone turned petulant.

"Every angel has a way to earn back their wings," Gabriel's voice swam through the group, cool and calm. "Cassiel's was to commit the ultimate act of sacrifice."

Paschar frowned. "What does that even mean?"

"I know it is something you would struggle to understand, *brother*," Trick said.

"It means he gave up his life, his existence, without thought of the consequences," Neemah glared. "He believed he would earn the final death through his actions, but acted anyway, to save the life of another."

"And who deserved this great honor?" Paschar's derision was clear.

Seraphina stepped forward. "I did."

Paschar finally noticed the gore-coated fallen angel. He paled.

"Seraphina...you didn't...you wouldn't..." Paschar finally seemed to get hold of himself. "How could you betray me in such a way?"

"Betray *you*?" Seraphina was incredulous.

What?

They were lovers. Gabriel's voice whispered in Trick's mind. *Paschar had proposed the day she lost her wings. He renounced her.*

Trick stared at the archangel. *Thank you.*

You are welcome. The dark-haired spy-master turned a fond gaze on Seraphina. *I always held a soft spot for her. I do not know what she saw in your brother.*

Half-brother.

A cool mental chuckle reached him, belying Gabriel's impassive face.

"Enough!" Hades shouted.

Paschar closed his mouth.

"Did you, or did you not find your brother healing a demon?" Uriel demanded.

"I did." Paschar drew himself up.

Truth.

"But had you kidnapped and raped her first?" Trick asked.

Paschar's face turned a dull red. "You do not get to ask questions, traitor."

Hades tapped his foot. "It's a valid question, don't you think?" He turned to Baal, who nodded. "I mean, where'd the demon come from first? Why was he healing her?"

"I found them together," Paschar said.

"Did you kidnap and rape the demon prior to Trick healing her?" Hades repeated, on Trick's behalf.

"I don't have to answer to you." Paschar refused to look at the god.

Neemah strode forward. "No, but you have to answer

to me."

"Lady Nanael, we are almost related. You know the evil in Cassiel's heart."

"You always were a jealous little worm." Her brown eyes flashed.

Rage made Paschar's lips thin. "Jealousy is a sin."

"Then why do you boil with it?" Hades asked. "Now, answer the question."

"His silence admits his guilt," Baal said. "Cut his wings off and be done with it."

Paschar spun. "Who are you? I am innocent of any wrongdoing."

Truth. But not truth.

Trick narrowed his eyes. "You honestly don't believe that kidnapping and raping demons is wrong?"

"Of course, it's not!" Paschar cried. "They are nothing but insects."

"So, you did it," Neemah said.

"I didn't say that."

How easily he dodges direct questions, Trick thought to his sister. She flashed him a look, then smiled. But it was a cold, cold expression. A blade of glittering starlight appeared in her hand. "Answer the question or lose your wings."

"No. This is a set-up."

"The only set-up was you framing your brother," Hades said. "Now admit it."

"Never." Paschar shook his head. "Cassiel deserves this."

Truth.

"What did I ever do to you?" Trick asked, curious despite himself.

Paschar whirled on him. "What did you ever do? The wonderful healer who could do no wrong? The calm one, the peaceful one? And then one day, I found a feather of yours with the first hints of gold. You didn't deserve to ascend. *I* did. I am the one with the talent, with the purpose."

That was it?

One thousand years of exile, all because his brother had set him up out of sheer jealousy—and the fact that Uriel had been so insecure, he was glad to see Trick lose his wings?

Exile is not a strong enough punishment for him, he thought at Seraphina. *He needs to suffer more.*

Uriel did, too, but he had no say in that.

Seraphina clasped his hand in hers, her palm sticky with blood. *No,* she said into his mind. *I have an idea.*

*We need to get you some help. All that blood on you…*He squeezed her hand.

It's all right, it's not mine. It's Lucifer's.

What???

CHAPTER 35

I will explain later, Seraphina replied.

Although, there wasn't much to explain.

She just wished she had finished the job. Not to mention that she was still reeling from the revelation that Trick had been a fallen *angel*.

She'd never have guessed, not in a thousand years.

And now he has his wings back. He will return to Heaven, and I will be stuck in Hell.

They would never see each other again.

I won't accept it.

She had been prepared to hunt him down beyond death, to try to bring him back: she wasn't going to give up on him now.

Trick's hand warmed in her palm, until it grew too hot to touch. She pulled away, but only after her skin had blistered.

He stared at her wound, then her face. "I did that?" His back bowed, and his jaw clenched so hard the tendons in his neck stood out in sharp relief.

What is happening? She asked telepathically, but there

was no response, just a burst of pain that made her nerve endings sizzle.

A bright light engulfed Trick, so intense she had to shield her eyes. He groaned as the illumination faded, leaving starbursts on her retina, and kneeled on the floor, his head bowed, wings shivering.

"Trick?" She stepped toward him, holding out her uninjured hand.

He looked up, then took the hand. Energy rushed through her and she was refreshed, healed. The burn was gone.

"You didn't have to do that."

He smiled gently. "I wanted to." Then he unfurled his wings.

Seraphina gasped.

In the background, Uriel cursed and Michael slammed his sword into the floor.

"They're pretty cool, huh?" Trick said.

"This is a travesty!" Paschar shouted.

"Oh, shut up." Hades flicked his hand, and Paschar stilled, his eyes glazing over, his mouth open in another retort.

Seraphina held out a wavering hand. "You're an archangel."

"He doesn't deserve it!" Uriel snarled. "He has been cavorting with demons for a thousand years."

"Only because you took his wings. You failed him, Uriel. You failed us." Neemah glared at her fellow archangel. "Our Lord has rectified your wrong."

"*My* wrong?" Uriel's eyes burned. He turned to Trick. "Keep out of my way. I am going to petition against this!"

The dark-skinned angel vanished, Michael following

in his wake.

"The others will have felt his ascension, but I will go spread the news." Gabriel met Seraphina's stare, dipped his head in acknowledgement, and disappeared.

That left Laird, Hades, Trick, Nanael and herself.

I am not worthy to be here.

The realization struck home.

Trick took her hand, running his thumb over her wrist, as if he sensed her discomfort.

An icy wind swept through the room, making her skin pebble. One of the walls grew transparent, and a figure became visible in the distance. Hades whistled low, while Lady Nanael frowned.

Who is it? Could it be...?

But no.

As the figure came closer, it became apparent it was a woman, her skin the color of death, and her sapphire-blue hair swept up high on her head. Dark blue tendrils snaked down over her shoulders, lying carelessly over her silver dress, which sparkled like it was embedded with diamonds.

A heartbeat later, she was in the room, her eyes black pools of darkness. Age and power exuded from her, battering at Seraphina's mind until she feared she might scream. Then the onslaught tempered, allowing her to breathe, her exhalations misty in the rapidly cooling air.

"My Lady." Hades bowed low.

Baal followed suit. "My Lady, it is always a pleasure to see you. But I fear I have other matters to attend to. If you'll excuse me." The god vanished.

The lady spoke, her voice cold, cold, cold. "He was always one to avoid lingering." Then she chuckled, the sound reminding Seraphina of skittering beetles.

I do not know who she is, but she is scary.

"You do not bow." She turned to Lady Nanael.

"You are not my god." The angel tilted her chin up.

"No, you are my sibling's creations. That is true." Those black eyes studied the archangel with intensity.

"Who are you?" Trick breathed.

"I have had many names. I am one, and I am all. But I was once fond of the term Ereshkigal."

"The Queen of the Underworld," Trick murmured.

"You know of me. Good." She smiled, exposing neat, tidy teeth, with slightly longer incisors.

A primordial god.

I am staring at a primordial god.

They rarely took on physical form, with the majority moving on to different worlds, different places.

"Why do you come here? This is not your realm." Lady Nanael clenched her fist.

"I am here for Cassiel."

"*Me?*" Trick's eyebrows rose.

"You have a choice. Heaven or Hell. You can stay here, but as an archangel, you will be bound to Heaven and its rules for eternity. Or, you can become a true fallen again, and live in Hell."

Trick tightened his grip on Seraphina's hand. "I don't want to lose my wings."

The goddess shook her head slowly, as if remembering body language from a long-ago era. "You won't need to."

He grinned. "Then it's easy. Hell."

"What! Cassiel, *no*." Lady Nanael shoved her way toward her brother. "You only just ascended. You need time to reacclimatize. We could get to know one another again."

"We could have gotten to know each other over the past thousand years. Yet you made no effort. The gold in my wings doesn't change who I am, who I've always been."

Seraphina's heart swelled to the point of bursting.

"What if *she* gets her wings back? You won't be able to see her again." Lady Nanael pointed at Seraphina.

"Then what happens next is her choice," Trick said. "I will not bind her to me."

"You enslaved her before," Hades commented.

"She offered herself for Z. And I only bought Z out of pity. Anyway, she is the majority owner of the Halcyon Guild now. No one owns her."

So, Sylvester was correct.

Her rush of power had not been fueled by her anger alone.

"She is a true fallen," Ereshkigal murmured. "Her return to Heaven will not be so simple."

"But she hasn't drunk the blood of a death god."

"Has she not?" Ereshkigal said, her eyes on Seraphina's lips.

Lips crusted with gore.

"I must have swallowed some of Lucifer's blood by accident."

"That is *Lucifer's* blood?" Lady Nanael demanded.

"Yes, I would have cut his head off, but Laird stopped me. I had almost done it."

"He was wise to do so," Ereshkigal said. "Sheol can only be ruled by another fallen angel, a death god, or his own progeny. There are few of those in the world.

Without Lucifer, there will be chaos."

The primordial god moved closer to Trick. "Have you chosen? If you do, you must drink my blood. Now you are an archangel, Hades' is not strong enough."

"Is there room in Hell for me?" he asked.

"Yes." Hades nodded. "I will make room."

Trick turned to the goddess. "Let's do this."

CHAPTER 36

Power buzzed through Trick's veins, the taste of frozen berries lingering on his tongue. Ereshkigal's blood did not remind him of death, rather—surprisingly—of fruit and laughter and life. His wings had turned the palest of grays—matching Ereshkigal's skin tone—while the gold stood out in stark relief.

The primordial god vanished, a strangely flirty smile on her lips. Now, he was left with his sister, Seraphina, and Hades. He wanted to kiss Seraphina silly, but he somewhat doubted she'd appreciate it while they had an audience.

She came for me.

She had thought he was dead, but she had come after him anyway.

No one else had cared enough about him to do so. Not even his sister, whose brown eyes echoed a deep hurt.

"You should have stayed, Cassiel," Neemah said. "Tried it for a little while."

"I would have wanted to kill Uriel too much. It's better this way."

"Uriel is older than you. You would have failed."

"But not stronger," Hades said. "Trick's ascension was a thousand years in the making. He's caught up and then some."

"I—" But Neemah seemed to change her mind. "What do we do about him?" She pointed at Paschar.

"I think we give him to Hades, as a gift for his Hall of Statues," Seraphina said.

Trick grinned, then rubbed his hands together gleefully. "Oh, that is a great idea."

"Hall of Statues?" Neemah asked.

"It's a place where I put people who piss me off. I turn them into gargoyles and leave them there. Some are aware, others aren't."

"He deserves to fall," Neemah said.

"I don't have an angel in my collection." Hades rubbed his jaw. "I now desperately have to have one. He's mine." The god clicked his fingers, and Paschar vanished.

"You do not get to dictate angel law!" Neemah cried.

"No, but I'm an archangel, and the one who was wronged by him," Trick said. "I say let Hades have him."

Neemah glowered. "You can tell your mother, then."

"Oh, I will. I am wondering what will upset her more, the fact I am an archangel or that her baby boy is now a gargoyle."

"Shouldn't she be upset he was a rapist and murderer?" Hades asked.

"You'd think so, but no." Trick shook his head.

The god narrowed his eyes. "You angels are fucked up."

"Yup."

"Cassiel—" Neemah held out a hand.

"Call me Trick," he said. "And come visit me once in a while, if you want."

The cloud room around them vanished, and they appeared in Hades' office. It was a tight fit, with Trick's wings. Hades bumped past them to his side of the desk, then sat with a sigh.

"Asha goes on leave for two weeks, and this happens. The paperwork alone is going to send me blind." He looked up at them. "Sit."

Trick spun his chair around and straddled it, arms resting against the back. Seraphina sat in a more traditional fashion.

Hades nodded. "Did you get the spear?"

"You can't seriously think that that contract still stands." Seraphina slammed her hand on his desk, making loose sheets of paper cascade to the floor. "You can't kill us, I won't allow it."

"You just ruined my filing system."

She jerked back. "*That* is a system?"

"Yes, we did it." Trick said, getting things back on track. He reached into his shirt and withdrew the *Amenonuhoko*. "I managed to swap it out just before Lucifer arrived."

Seraphina's jaw dropped.

"Perfect." Hades held out a hand.

"Why do you want it, anyway?" Trick passed the artifact over.

Hades sighed. "Ereshkigal came to me, and said I had to give you a task, a task which involved you going before Lucifer. She said I had to make sure you did it, threaten you with death if need be. You don't say no to primordial gods. Ever."

"Do you think she saw this outcome?" Seraphina asked.

"Probably."

Trick frowned. "But why the *Amenonuhoko*?"

"Because I know someone who'd love it, and whose anniversary is coming up." Hades turned to Seraphina. "Go get clean. I have a few words I want to say to Trick."

"Is there a bathroom around here?" she asked.

Hades waved a hand, and she disappeared.

"You love doing that."

"Damn right I do." The god laughed, but he quickly sobered. "Tartarus isn't a big place, Trick. Hell is...static, shall we say. But I know someone who can wield the *Amenonuhoko*."

It all clicked into place.

"Asha. She can create more land. More Tartarus."

Hades gave him the thumbs up. "Bingo."

"Will she want to?"

"Man, she will be able to create her ideal landmass. She'll make me build her a fortress. She'll love it. And it's a great ten-year anniversary present."

"I thought she just worked for you."

"She does. But you don't forget things like anniversary dates when your second-in-command is a death goddess."

"*You're* a death god."

"And I want to stay that way."

"Right." The conversation was beginning to make little sense.

Hades pocketed the *Amenonuhoko*. "If you want to stay in Tartarus, you will need to swear fealty to the realm."

"Sure."

"Bold move, making Seraphina your heir."

Trick shrugged.

"You might want to check she hasn't drowned." Hades smirked, and Trick reappeared in a bathroom. It was huge, and well-appointed, with mosaic walls and floor, a sunken tub with a solid gold faucet, and luxuriously soft towels. The polished stone counter went for miles, and had two sinks, while the shower could fit three people—or two, if one had wings.

Seraphina was in the shower, and she spun, startled at his appearance. She had already palmed a knife—where did she keep that? —and was ready to strike before she recognized him.

"Trick."

"Seraphina."

He stepped under the spray with her, clothes and all. She pressed herself to him. "I thought you were dead. I *saw* you die. I *felt* it."

Tears, hot and wet hit his neck, and his heart squeezed. "I would die a million times to make sure you survived."

She raised her head, the blood gone from her face. "And I would die a million times for you."

"We're at a stalemate then."

"I almost killed Lucifer for hurting you. I would have, if Laird hadn't intervened." Her brown eyes were molten as she stared at him.

"No one has ever done such a nice thing for me before."

She punched him in the arm. "Can you ever be serious?"

"Yes."

"When?" she demanded.

"When I am making love to you."

"Making love? Is that what you call it?"

"Yep."

"Is that your way of saying you love me?" She frowned.

"Yep."

"Trick!" She put him in a headlock.

"Hey! No fair. I'm the healer angel. Don't take advantage of me."

"Aren't you meant to be taking advantage of me?" she asked lasciviously.

He laughed, delighted in her. In them.

"Don't you love me?" Trick asked, his voice slightly taunting. "You nearly killed the ruler of Sheol cos he stabbed me a little."

"Stabbed you a little? You were *dead*!"

"Way to avoid answering."

She pressed a kiss against his lips, hot and needy and demanding all at once. "Does that answer your question?"

"No, I don't think it does."

"Stubborn archangel."

"Vengeful guild master."

They kissed again, long and slow and passionate.

"Do you mind that I made you my heir?" He asked, pulling away. He had to know she wasn't angry at him for it.

"It came as a surprise. Why did you do it?"

"I figured you would make a great leader. And you didn't try and kill my assassins when you first met them.

You'd be fair. Level-headed. What the guild needed."

"When did you do it? After we slept together?"

"Before. The day after you joined."

He'd seen her potential from the start. Had known the decision was right. "I knew that you'd look after them if I died."

"Enough talk of death. How about we both live? For each other?" She licked water from her lips, drawing his eyes back to the lush contours.

"For each other."

CHAPTER 37

Yael glared at the Djinn.

"I don't give a fuck if you're Lucifer himself, I know she's here." He could feel Dina's presence at the Casa de los Condenados. Not in the tap room, which was filled with all kinds of demons, but somewhere in the building.

The giant Djinn on the other side of the bar ground his jaw. "Look, I don't know what it is with you fallen angel types, but get the fuck out of my bar."

Yael cracked his knuckles. He was dying for a good fight.

"That's okay, Lamar. I will see him."

He turned towards the clipped voice. There, just visible through a door that led into the kitchens, was Dina, so beautiful it almost hurt to look at her, with golden hair swept back, and crystalline eyes so pure they reminded him of endless blue skies.

"Go outside," the Djinn grumbled.

"Thanks," Yael muttered, then elbowed his way through the crowd to the front door.

I found her, I found her.

I fucking found her.

But why was she free, when Z had been tortured, mutilated?

Once outside, the sulfuric stink seeped into his lungs.

"Yael." Dina's voice reached him from the corner of the stone building.

Carefully, he headed over to where she stood, half-covered in shade. Her posture was regal and straight, her face set in its customary harsh lines. Behind her spread two dark appendages, their black so deep they appeared as nothing more than shadows.

"Dina, you're alive."

"You always were good at stating the obvious." Her voice was flat, unwelcoming.

"We've been looking for you for months." Using every contact they had.

"You obviously weren't looking too hard. I've been here for months."

He winced.

"Then why didn't you try and contact us? Surely you heard..."

"I heard."

"Then why stay here? In Hell?"

She stepped forward, out of the darkness. Her wings were horrifyingly beautiful. *A black-winged angel. I have never seen such a thing.*

"Because I want to be here. Go home. Leave. Don't come back for me, Yael. You'll just be wasting your time."

But he wasn't ready to give up. "What happened? Did they take you, too?"

"Go, Yael. And tell the others I'm done with the Darts." Dina turned her back on him and walked away.

Foolish.

He reached forward to grab her shoulder, but she spun, lightning fast. "Last warning." Something dangerous swirled to life within Dina's gaze, malevolence shooting from her.

"Fine." He ripped his hand from her hold and stalked toward the front of the Casa de los Condenados.

Dina doesn't want to join us.

Fine.

We don't need her.

Time to tell the others.

CHAPTER 38

Seraphina smiled at Trick, then Raze. They stood outside the recreation room at Raze's mansion. "Raze, this is Trick. I'm not sure you've formally met before."

"Raziel. Ex-scholar-turned-warrior. I've heard of you." Trick held out his hand.

"And I you, Cassiel." Raze clasped the new archangel's hand in his.

"I prefer Trick."

The dark-skinned angel with the storm-colored eyes nodded.

As they stepped into the room, a blade spun through the air to thwack into a wall. Seraphina glared. She'd had enough flying daggers to last her a lifetime.

This time, however, there was no threat, just Azrael engaged in a knife-throwing competition with Dru. According to Raze, they had been arguing over who was the better throw for the past month.

They clearly haven't met Lucifer.

The recreation room at Raze's mansion was huge, with a massive TV, sofa, pool table, and bar. There was even a target on one wall, for Azrael and Dru's competition. Z was in the room, sitting on a backless sofa with a tumbler of whiskey in his hand. And in the center, Yale stood, brooding.

"You found Dina?" Seraphina asked.

"I did," Yael said, then stopped as he spotted Trick. "Who the fuck is that?"

Dru dropped her dagger. "Trick!"

Azrael yelped and darted out the way. "Watch out!"

The female assassin dashed forward, coming to a stop bare inches from her former boss. "You're a fucking archangel! Who did you kill for that to happen?"

"I didn't kill anyone," Trick answered.

"He died," Seraphina said, her expression solemn.

Yael's mental voice reached her. *Tell me you didn't...tell me you didn't sleep with the guild master.*

Seraphina shot him a glare. *He gave his life for me.*

Dru whooped. "You! It was you!" She was pointing at Seraphina.

"It was her what?" Azrael asked.

"There's rumors someone almost cut off Lucifer's head. Their description matches Seraphina. And look at her. She's got an evil-type vibe going now." The cambion's gray eyes were almost glowing.

Seraphina bit her lip.

I give off an evil vibe? she asked Trick telepathically.

Comes with being a true fallen. It was how I could mask I was an angel, he replied.

"I can't admit to anything," Seraphina said, holding up her hands.

"Oh, yes! This is great. You have to tell me *everything*." Dru grabbed her arm and tugged her toward the sofa.

"Most women act that way when they talk about lovers, not murdering people," Trick muttered.

"I am not most women." Dru sniffed.

"Hear, hear," Azrael said.

Dru flipped Azrael the bird; he blew her a kiss.

They're relationship is weird, Seraphina sent to Trick.

What? You put me in a headlock yesterday.

You deserved it.

True.

"Are you all fucking insane? Didn't you hear me? *I found Dina.*" Yael's voice growled through the room.

"Where is she?" Dru demanded.

"At the Casa de los Condenados," Yael replied. "She has black wings. She looks healthy. Healthy and mean."

"I knew it," Seraphina muttered.

That black feather.

"Let's go get her," Z said, standing. He finished his whiskey in one large mouthful.

Yael scuffed his foot. "Ah, that's the thing."

"What?"

"She says to leave her alone, she's done with the Darts."

Silence.

"She's *what*?"

"She said that?"

"What the fuck?"

It was hard to keep track of who said what.

Dina was a force to be reckoned with back when I was in Heaven, Trick said to her telepathically. *If she doesn't want to come join you, she won't.*

I know, Seraphina replied.

"Do you think she was part of it, then?" Dru asked.

"Part of what?" Yael snapped.

"Well, Z got tortured, you all fell, and she's all fine and dandy." Dru spun another knife through her fingers. "She has her wings, and she's free. Do you think she helped the demons break into Heaven?"

Yael looked uncertain. "I—I have no idea."

I can't believe Dina would do that.

Then again, I didn't think Paschar was a psychopath who tortured demons for fun. Her former lover had hated blood; he'd made her wash it off whenever she'd been in a battle.

Or maybe he'd done that because he liked it too much.

She still hadn't come to terms with Paschar's true nature. Or the fact he was Trick's half-brother. That would take time.

"We still have to find two pieces of the Heart," Raze said, pouring himself a whiskey. "In the meantime, let's try and learn about Dina's role in the whole affair."

Azrael nodded. "Agreed."

"I sure as Hell would like to know," Z growled. "I still have some debts to pay back." He cracked his knuckles, the poisonous jade-green filaments in his wings catching the light.

They broke off into groups, talking amongst themselves. Trick caught her hand, holding it tight. "Will you tell them?" *That you can't go back?*

"Soon." But for now, she would enjoy their company. And she would take each day as it came.

"Do you think Lucifer will search for me?" she asked.

"Your Hades' ward. He can't." Trick set his jaw. "And he'd have to get through me first."

"You say the most romantic things."

He laughed, the sound warm and vibrant, and wonderful. "I do. Want to put me in a headlock later?"

EPILOGUE

Dina stared at the incriminating feather in her hand. It was tiny, so tiny.

Like most people's lives.

She crushed it in a strong grip, then threw it in the fire and watched it burn, curling in on itself, withering to nothing.

So, there was a new archangel in Tartarus. Meanwhile, Lucifer was said to be pissed beyond Hell after nearly being decapitated, Hades was gloating with some private victory, and Satan was being his usual diabolical self.

Dina barred her teeth in a mockery of a smile. "Look out boys, it's my turn to play."

Acknowledgements

Winged Passion was a fun book to write, done madly during my newborn daughter's naps. As usual, there are plenty of people who deserve thanks. Firstly, I'd like to thank my husband Tom, who gave me the time to write this book, while we juggled our three-month-old daughter's needs. I also want to thank my wonderful beta readers Joanne Danton and Kel Carpenter, and my eagle-eyed editor Pete Kempshall. As always, you are invaluable in the creation of my work.

Amanda Pillar is an USA TODAY Bestselling Author and award-winning editor who lives in Victoria, Australia, with her husband, daughter, and two cats.

Amanda has had numerous short stories published and has co-edited six fiction anthologies and solo-edited two.

Amanda's first novel, *Graced*, was published by Momentum in 2015. The stories *Captive* and *Survivor* were also released in 2016, followed by *Bitten* and *Ashes* in 2017. She has also just launched the Heaven's Heart series.

In her day job, she works as an archaeologist.

www.ingramcontent.com/pod-product-compliance
Lightning Source LLC
Chambersburg PA
CBHW021420110726
47901CB00008B/2232